Praise for Yu Hua's

THE SEVENTH DAY

"Plaintive. . . . Moving." —*Grantland*

"A ghostly walk through contemporary China evokes the human cost of some of the big issues that nation is facing." —*Toronto Star*

"Mesmerizing. . . . Internationally award-winning novelist [Yu] crafts a discerning critique of contemporary Chinese culture through an evocative allegory revealing fates much worse than death." —*Booklist*

"[A] poignant fable about family bonds made not of blood ties but unbreakable heartstrings. It will assuredly reward Yu's readers, familiar and new."

—*Library Journal* (starred review)

Yu Hua
THE SEVENTH DAY

Yu Hua is the author of five novels, six story collections, and three essay collections. His work has been translated into more than twenty languages. He is the recipient of many awards, including the James Joyce Award, France's Prix Courrier International, and Italy's Premio Grinzane Cavour. Yu Hua lives in Beijing.

Allan H. Barr is the translator of Yu Hua's debut novel, *Cries in the Drizzle*, his essay collection *China in Ten Words*, and his short-story collection *Boy in the Twilight*. He teaches Chinese at Pomona College in California.

ALSO BY YU HUA

Boy in the Twilight

China in Ten Words

Brothers

Cries in the Drizzle

Chronicle of a Blood Merchant

To Live

The Past and the Punishments

THE
SEVENTH
DAY

A Novel

Yu Hua

Translated from the Chinese by Allan H. Barr

ANCHOR BOOKS
A Division of Penguin Random House LLC
New York

FIRST ANCHOR BOOKS EDITION, JANUARY 2016

The Library of Congress has cataloged the Pantheon edition as follows:
Yu, Hua.
[880-01 Diqi tian. English]
The seventh day : a novel / Yu Hua ; translated from the Chinese by
Allan H. Barr.
pages cm
I. Barr, Allan Hepburn, translator.   II. Title.   III. Title: 7th day.
PL2928.H78D513 2014   895.13'52—dc23   2014018468

Anchor Books Trade Paperback ISBN: 978-0-8041-7205-9
eBook ISBN: 978-0-8041-9787-8

Book design by Iris Weinstein

www.anchorbooks.com

Printed in the United States of America
10   9   8   7

THE
SEVENTH
DAY

THE FIRST DAY

The fog was thick when I left my bedsit and ventured out alone into the barren and murky city. I was heading for what used to be called a crematorium and these days is known as a funeral parlor. I had received a notice instructing me to arrive by 9:00 a.m., because my cremation was scheduled for 9:30.

The night before had resounded with the sounds of collapsing masonry—one huge crash after another, as though a whole line of buildings was too tired to stay standing and had to lie down. In this continual bedlam I drifted fitfully between sleep and wakefulness. At daybreak, when I opened the door, the din suddenly halted, as though just by opening the door I had turned off the switch that controlled the noise. On the door a slip had been posted next to the notices that had been taped there ten days earlier, asking me to pay the electricity and water bills. In characters damp and blurry in the fog, the new notice instructed me to proceed to the funeral parlor for cremation.

Fog had locked the city into a single, unchanging guise, erasing the boundaries between day and night, morning and evening. As I walked toward the bus stop, several human figures appeared out of nowhere, only to disappear just as quickly. I cautiously walked ahead for a distance, but found my passage blocked by some kind of sign that appeared to have suddenly grown out of the ground. I thought there ought to be some numbers on it—if the number 203 was there, then this was the stop for the bus I wanted to take. But I couldn't make out the numbers, even when I felt for them with my hand. When I rubbed my eyes, I seemed to see the number 203, suggesting that this was indeed the stop. But now I had a strange feeling that while my right eye was in the original place, my left eye had moved outward to my cheekbone. Then I became aware that next to my nose a foreign object had attached itself to my face, and something else was caught underneath my chin. When I felt around with my hand, I discovered that my nose was next to my nose and my chin next to my chin—somehow they had altered their locations.

The fog was now even more dense. Amid the murky figures and ghostly buildings I heard sounds of life rising and falling like ripples of water. Then, as I took a few tentative steps farther on, hoping to penetrate the gloom, I heard cars crashing into each other. The fog had drenched my eyes and I couldn't see the collisions—all I was aware of was a series of violent impacts. A car burst out of the fog behind me and sped past and into the sounds of life, and the sounds churned and popped like boiling water.

I stood there uncertainly for a little while, but soon realized that if there was a pileup on this stretch of road, the No. 203 bus would not arrive anytime soon and I should go on to the next stop.

As I walked on ahead, snowflakes came billowing out of the fog. They seemed to glow like patches of light, and when they landed on my face, my skin felt slightly warmer. I stood still, watching the snowflakes fall through the air and settle on me. My clothes gradually stood out more clearly against the snow.

This was an important day, I realized—my first day of death. I hadn't washed and I hadn't dressed in funerary costume—I was simply wearing my ordinary clothes, with a baggy old overcoat on top, as I headed toward the funeral parlor. Stricken with sudden misgivings at my sloppy attire, I turned on my heel and headed back in the direction from which I'd come.

The falling snow had brought some light to the city and the thick fog seemed to slowly dissipate as I walked, so that I could faintly make out pedestrians and vehicles going to and fro. As I reached the bus stop I had left shortly before, a scene of utter confusion met my eyes: the road was completely blocked by a chaotic tangle of over twenty vehicles, with police cars and ambulances ringing the perimeter. There were people lying on the ground and others being pulled from cars that were twisted completely out of shape; there were people moaning and people crying and people who made no sound at all. I stopped for a minute, and this time I could see clearly the number 203 on the sign. I made my way past.

When I got back to my bedsit, I undressed, walked naked over to the shower enclosure, and turned on the faucet. As I filled my palms with water and began to wash, I found that my body was covered in wounds, and I gingerly removed the bits of gravel and splinters of wood that were embedded in the open lesions.

Just then my mobile phone started to ring. I found this strange, because service had been disconnected two months earlier for nonpayment, and here suddenly it was ringing again. I picked it up and pressed the listen button. "Hello?" I said quietly.

A voice responded. "Is that Yang Fei?"

"That's right."

"Funeral parlor here. Where are you now?"

"I'm at home."

"What are you doing?"

"I'm washing."

"It's almost nine o'clock now! How can you still be washing?"

"I'll be there soon." I felt embarrassed.

"Hurry up, then, and be sure to bring your reservation slip."

"Where will I find that?"

"It'll be on your door."

Then the caller hung up. I wasn't very happy about this—why was there such a rush? I put down the phone and renewed my efforts to clean my wounds. I picked up a bowl, filled it with water, and used it to wash out the remaining grit and splinters. This helped to speed things up.

Still dripping wet, I walked over to the wardrobe and opened it, in search of a funerary costume. But I could find nothing answering this description; the closest thing was a pair of white silk pajamas with a low-key flower pattern and the characters, now faded, that Li Qing had embroidered in red thread on the chest—a souvenir of my brief marriage. She had carefully chosen two pairs of traditional Chinese-style pajamas for us one day, and had sewn my name on hers and her name on mine. I had never worn these pajamas since our marriage broke up, but now, when I put them on once more, their color seemed as warm as that of snow.

I opened the door and carefully studied the funeral parlor notice posted on the outside. On the slip was written A3—a reservation number, by the look of it—so I detached it, folded it carefully, and put it in my pajama pocket.

As I was about to leave, I had the feeling I'd forgotten

something and stood for a moment in the swirling snow to ponder. Then I remembered—a black armband. I was a single man, parentless and childless, with nobody to come and mourn my passing, so it was up to me to wear one.

I went back into my room and riffled through the wardrobe for some black cloth. After a prolonged search all I could find was a black shirt so worn that it was now turning gray. I cut off part of the sleeve and placed it over my left arm. My mourning attire clearly left something to be desired, but I felt tolerably satisfied with the effect.

Once more my phone rang. "Is that Yang Fei?"

"Yes, hello."

"Funeral parlor here. Are you still planning to get cremated?"

I hesitated for a moment. "Yes, I am."

"It's nine-thirty now—you're late."

"Is it so important to be on time?" I wanted to do things right.

"If you want to get cremated, you need to hurry it up."

Entering the funeral parlor, I found the waiting room spacious and deep. The fog outside had gradually dissipated but the waiting room itself was still wreathed in mist, and some widely spaced wall sconces in the shape of candles gave off a pale glow, also the shade of snow. Somehow I felt warmed by the color white.

The right side of the waiting room was taken up by rows of plastic chairs bolted to the floor, while on the left side was an armchair zone with chairs arranged in several rings and with plastic flowers laid out on the coffee table in the center of each circle. On the plastic chairs many people were waiting, but there were only five seated in the armchairs. Those in the armchairs sat comfortably, with a foot resting on the opposite knee, looking very pleased with their accomplishments, while everyone in the rows of plastic seats sat stiffly and properly.

As I entered, a man wearing a faded blue jacket and a pair of old gloves walked toward me. He was so thin that his bones were like sticks and his face seemed little more than a skull, for it had hardly any skin and flesh.

Seeing my face with its altered features, he greeted me softly. "Good morning, sir."

"Is this the crematorium?" I asked.

"It's not called the crematorium anymore," he said. "It's called the funeral parlor."

I realized I'd said the wrong thing, a bit like entering a hotel and asking, "Is this the hostel?"

In his voice I detected a weary, jaded tone, and I could tell he was not the person who had called from the funeral parlor earlier. I apologized for my tardiness, but he shook his head gently and consoled me by informing me that late arrivals were not unusual. My reservation number had expired and was no longer valid, so he walked over to the number-dispensing machine at the entrance to pick up a new ticket for me.

I had been pushed back from A3 to A64; according to the ticket, I had fifty-four people ahead of me.

"Will you be able to fit me in today?" I asked.

"There are always some no-shows," the usher replied.

With a gloved finger he pointed at the plastic chairs to indicate that was where I should wait. Noticing that my eyes were drawn to the armchairs, he explained that they belonged to the VIP zone, and my status qualified me only for a place in the basic seating. As I made my way, ticket in hand, over to the plastic chairs, I heard him muttering to himself, "Another poor guy who's come here without a face-lift."

I sat down on a plastic chair. The usher paced back and forth in the pathway that separated the two waiting areas, seemingly lost in thought, his shoes tapping on the floor with the same steady rhythm as that of someone knocking on a door. Late arrivals kept showing up, and he would greet them and hand them a reservation ticket and point a finger in the direction of the plastic chairs. One of the late arrivals was an elite guest, and the usher walked him over to the armchair zone.

The crematees on the plastic chairs talked in low voices among themselves, while the six in the VIP area also chatted, but loudly, like singers projecting lyrics onstage. Our conversations were more like an accompaniment from the orchestra pit.

Funerary clothes and cinerary urns were the central topics of discussion among the VIPs. They were wearing exquisite handmade silk cerements with bright hand-embroidered designs, and they were discussing casually the price of these garments—all of which cost over twenty thousand yuan. The costumes looked splendid to me, like outfits worn in an imperial palace. Then the VIPs switched their attention to their respective cinerary urns, which were made of large-leaf red sandalwood engraved with exquisite designs and priced in the sixty-thousand-yuan range. The urns' names were equally splendid and imposing: Sandalwood Precincts, Immortal Crane Manor, Dragon Palace, Phoenix Castle, Unicorn Palace, and Sandalwood Mansion.

We commoners were discussing the same topics. In our case the funerary garments were of synthetic silk with cotton trim, and they cost about a thousand yuan. The cinerary urns were either cypress or wood composite, undecorated, the most expensive costing eight hundred yuan, the cheapest two hundred. The names for these urns took simpler forms, such as Falling Leaves Return to Their Roots, or Fragrance Lingering for Time Everlasting.

Whereas the VIP section was focused on the relative expense of the crematees' garments and urns, among the plastic chairs the focus was more on who got the best value for the money. Two crematees sitting in front of me found that they had bought identical sets of burial clothes at the same shop, but one had paid fifty yuan less than the other. The one who'd been charged more heaved a sigh. "My wife is hopeless at bargaining," he muttered to himself.

I noticed that the other crematees in the plastic seats were all wearing funeral garments, either traditional cerements in Ming-Qing style or contemporary designs in Mao-jacket idiom or Western fashion. I was the only one dressed in a pair of Chinese clasp-fastened pajamas, but I was glad that I had at least jettisoned the baggy cotton overcoat—although my white pajamas were shabby, they could scrape by here among the plastic seats.

But I had no urn, not even a cheap one like Falling Leaves or Fragrance Lingering. This issue began to vex me—just where would my ashes end up? Should they be scattered in the boundless ocean, perhaps? But that was out of the question. That's the resting place for the ashes of the great, with an airplane to carry them and a navy warship to guard the route, the ashes consigned to the sea amid the tears and sobs of relatives and underlings. My ashes would be tipped out of the oven and greeted with a broom and dustpan, then dumped in a garbage can.

An elderly gentleman on one of the adjacent chairs turned his head and looked at me in surprise. "You haven't washed or reshaped?"

"I washed," I said. "I did it myself."

"But what about your face?" he said. "The left eye has come out and your nose has got out of position and your chin is so long."

I realized now, to my chagrin, that I had forgotten about my face when washing. "I didn't reshape," I said.

"Your family really has been remiss," the old man said. "They neglected both the wash and the reshape."

In fact, of course, I was all alone. My adoptive father, Yang Jinbiao, who had raised me from infancy, had left me more than a year earlier when he realized he was terminally ill, and my birth parents were far away in a northern city, not realizing that at this moment I was already in another world.

A woman on the other side, who had been following our conversation all this time, now studied my outfit. "How come your cerements look like pajamas?" she asked.

"What I'm wearing is funerary garments," I explained.

"Funerary garments?" She didn't seem to understand.

"Funerary garments are the same things as cerements," the gentleman said. " 'Cerement' sounds better."

I noticed that their faces were heavily made up, as though they were about to perform onstage, rather than be cremated.

Someone else in the plastic seats began to complain to the usher. "I've been waiting for ages now, but I've yet to hear my number called."

"They're just in the middle of the farewell ceremony for the mayor," the usher replied. "They stopped after the first three crematees this morning and we need to wait for the mayor to enter the oven. It won't be your turn until he comes out."

"Why do you have to wait for him to be cremated before you do us?" the man continued to wrangle.

"I don't know the answer to that."

"How many ovens have you got?" another person waiting asked.

"Two—one import and one domestic-brand. The import is reserved for VIPs—you'll be using the domestic make."

"Is the mayor a VIP?"

"Yes."

"Does he need both ovens?"

"He'll be using the imported one."

"Well, why are you holding back on the domestic one, then?"

"I'm not clear about that—all I know is that both ovens are currently out of service."

A VIP in the armchair zone waved a hand to beckon the usher, who walked briskly over to attend to his inquiry.

"How long is it till the farewell to the mayor?" the VIP asked.

"I'm not quite sure." The usher paused. "It'll be a little while yet, I imagine. Please just wait patiently."

A crematee who had just arrived provided an update as he made his way to his seat. "If you add up all the city officials, big and small, as well as those from adjacent districts and counties, that must amount to over a thousand people, and every one of them needs to say goodbye to him, and they can't walk fast—they need to walk past slowly, and some will want to weep as well."

"What's so special about a mayor?" the VIP grumbled.

The new arrival had not finished. "Starting this morning, all the main roads in the city were sealed off and the vehicle carrying the mayor's remains moved along at walking pace, with several hundred cars following to escort it. What should have taken just thirty minutes required a good hour and a half. The main roads are still sealed off and regular traffic won't resume until after the mayor's ashes have been returned home."

If the main roads are sealed off, the other streets are bound to be crammed with traffic. I remembered the sound of collisions when I was walking in the fog that morning and the scene of havoc that I saw later. Then I was reminded of the news of the mayor's sudden death that had circulated in all the newspapers and on television channels a couple of weeks earlier. The official explanation was that the mayor had suffered a heart attack as a result of overwork; the popular version making the rounds on the Internet was that the mayor had suffered a heart attack in the executive suite of a five-star hotel just as he reached orgasm with a young model. The model was so shocked that she ran into the corridor screaming and sobbing, forgetting she was naked below the waist.

Then both sets of conversations turned to the topic of burial plots. Those in the plastic seats had plots measuring one square yard, whereas the burial grounds for the VIPs were all at least six acres. Perhaps because the VIPs had heard what the plastic-seaters were saying, one of them asked loudly, "How can one possibly make do with one square yard?"

A hush fell over the plastic seats as people began to listen to the luxurious appointments of those in the armchairs. Five out of the six burial plots were established on mountain peaks, facing the sea, encircled by clouds, the most uplifting and awe-inspiring ocean-view grave sites imaginable. The sixth was in a dale where trees grew thickly, streams gurgled, and birds sang, and where a natural rock that had been rooted there for hundreds of thousands of years served as headstone. These days everyone wants to eat organic food-stuffs, the owner said, but his was an organic headstone. Of the other five burial plots, two had monuments that were miniature versions of real buildings—one a Chinese-style courtyard dwelling, the other a Western-style villa—while two others boasted formal grave steles: they didn't go in for all that showy stuff, their owners said. The last one took everybody by surprise, for the stele was a full-scale replica of the Monument to the People's Heroes in Tiananmen Square, the only difference being that the inscription in Mao Zedong's calligraphy on the monument, "In eternal trib-ute to the people's heroes," had been changed to "In eter-nal tribute to Comrade Li Feng"—also in Mao's calligraphy, since the owner's family had hunted down the characters for "Comrade Li Feng" in Mao's manuscripts, enlarged them, and inscribed them on the stele.

"Comrade Li Feng—that's me," the owner added.

"It all sounds a bit risky," another VIP said. "One of these days the government might insist on demolishing a memo-rial like that."

"I've already paid my hush money," he responded confi-dently. "I can't afford to let the story get out, so my family has already deployed a dozen people to keep reporters from covering it. Twelve is exactly the strength of an army squad, and with a team of guards protecting me I can rest without any worries."

At this point the two rows of ceiling lights in the waiting room came on, and the twilight hour suddenly was trans-formed into noonday. The usher quickly marched toward the front door.

The mayor entered, dressed in a black suit, white shirt, and black tie. He walked in soberly, sporting heavy makeup on his face, a pair of bushy black eyebrows, and bright lipstick on his lips. The usher greeted him, leading him in solicitously. "Mayor, please make yourself comfortable in the VIP luxury suite."

The mayor, nodding, followed him in. Two huge doors in the waiting room slowly swung open, only to close again slowly once he had entered.

The VIPs in the armchairs had all gone quiet. The VIP luxury suite had reduced the armchair zone to silence; wealth conceded its inferiority to power.

Among the plastic chairs, conversation continued to rise and fall, with burial remaining the topic of interest. Everyone bemoaned the fact that graves were now even more expensive than houses. In graveyards that were terribly crowded, despite their remote location, a square-yard plot still cost you thirty thousand yuan—and with a guaranteed tenure of only twenty-five years. Although houses were expensive, at least you could be sure of keeping them for seventy years. Some crematees were highly indignant, while others were racked with anxiety. "What will happen after twenty-five years?" they worried. By that time the price of a grave plot would most likely have reached astronomical levels, and if their family couldn't afford to pay out for a renewal of the lease, their ashes would simply end up as fertilizer.

"Dying is such an expensive business these days!" one of the crematees in the front row grumbled.

"Best not to think about the future," the old gentleman next to me calmly advised.

The old man told me that seven years earlier he had purchased a square-yard plot for three thousand yuan, and now it was worth thirty thousand. He rejoiced in his foresight at the time—if he wanted to buy it now, he would never be able to afford it.

"In seven years the price has risen tenfold," he sighed.

Reservation numbers began to be called. The mayor had now been cremated, and his urn, over which the Communist Party flag had been laid, was deposited on a black hearse, which then slowly moved away, followed by several hundred sedans. Funereal music began to sound from the sealed-off roads. I realized now that whereas ordinary reservation numbers began with an A, VIP reservation numbers began with a V. I wasn't sure what letter reservation numbers of luxury VIPs like the mayor started with—perhaps they didn't require any number whatsoever.

The six VIPs with the V numbers went in. Many A numbers were called, but just as the usher in blue had said, there were a lot of no-shows—occasionally there would be ten or more no-shows one after another. I noticed now that the usher was standing in the passageway next to me, and when I raised my head to look at him, his weary voice again sounded. "The no-shows don't have graves."

I had neither urn nor grave. Why did I come here? I wondered.

I heard the number A64—my number—called, but I stayed put in my chair. A64 was called three times, and then they moved on to A65. The woman next to me stood up. She was wearing a traditional shroud—in the Qing dynasty style, it looked like—and as she walked, her wide sleeves swung back and forth.

The old man next to me was still waiting, and still chatting. He said that although his grave site was out of the way and hard to get to, the scenery was decent, with a small lake nearby and some just-planted saplings. He said that once he was there he planned to stay put, so it didn't matter to him that it was far away and not convenient to reach. Then he inquired in which funeral garden he would find my grave.

I shook my head. "I have no grave."

"Without a grave, where will you go?" he asked in astonishment.

I felt my body stand up. It took me and left the waiting room.

꒳

Once more I placed myself in the enveloping fog and swirling snow, but I didn't know where to go. I was stricken with uncertainty, knowing I had died but not knowing how.

I walked in a hazy, indistinct city, my thoughts searching for a direction to follow amid the densely intersecting paths of memory. I needed to track down the last scene in my life, I realized, and this final scene was bound to lie at the farthest end of one such path; finding it would mean I had identified the moment of my own death. Taking their cue from my body's motion, my thoughts traversed a myriad of scenes that swirled in profusion like so many snowflakes before finally arriving at one particular day.

This day seemed a lot like yesterday, or a lot like the day before, or perhaps it was today. The only thing I could be sure of was that it was my last day on earth. I saw myself walking down a road with a cold wind blowing in my face.

꒳

I was walking, walking toward the square in front of the city government headquarters. About two hundred people were standing there, protesting against forced demolitions. They had not, however, unfurled protest banners and were not shouting slogans—they were simply swapping stories of personal misfortune. From what I could make out as I made my way through their ranks, they had all in various ways fallen afoul of recent demolitions. An old lady with tears running down her face was saying that she had just left her house to buy groceries and returned to find her house was gone—she had thought for a moment that she had taken a wrong turn. Others were relating the terror they had experienced during late-night demolitions, when they were woken from sleep by huge blasts, their house swaying back and forth as though in an earthquake; only when they rushed out in panic did they see bulldozers and excavators destroying their housing complex. One man was loudly relating an embarrassing experience: just as he and his girlfriend were making love, their front door suddenly opened with a crash and several fierce-looking men burst in, tied them up inside their comforter, and then carried them, comforter and all, into a waiting vehicle. It drove around the city the whole night, with him and his girlfriend scared out of their wits, not knowing where they were being taken. Only at dawn did the car return them to their place of departure; at that point their captors dumped them on the ground, untied the cord that bound them, and tossed them some items of clothing. Shivering, they hastily dressed, as passersby watched them curiously, and when they finally stood up and looked around they found that their home had been flattened. His girlfriend burst out wailing and vowed never to go to bed with him again—sleeping with him was scarier than watching a horror movie.

With the house gone and his girlfriend gone, he told the people around him, his sexual desire had completely dried up. He stretched out four fingers. In an effort to cure his erectile dysfunction, he said, he had already spent over forty thousand yuan and consumed all kinds of Western and Chinese medicines and resorted to remedies both orthodox and unconventional, but down below, his plane was only capable of taxiing.

"Does it start its descent just after taking off?" someone asked.

"Oh, I wish," he said. "No, it taxis only, no taking off at all."

"Demand compensation!" someone shouted.

"The government compensated me for my demolished house"—he smiled grimly—"but not for my traumatized libido."

"Take some Viagra," someone suggested.

"I did that," he said, "and it made my heart pound sure enough, but down below all I could do was taxi."

Much laughter followed this remark; it seemed to me that these people weren't protesting so much as having a party. After crossing the square, I passed two bus stops; ahead of me was Amity Street.

My life was at a low ebb by this point: my wife had left me long before, and more than a year earlier my father had fallen gravely ill. So as to pay for his treatment and look after him better, I had sold our apartment, handed in my notice, and bought a little shop near the hospital. Later, my father left without saying goodbye and disappeared in the endless sea of people, so I gave up the shop and moved into a cheap rental, searching for my father despite all the odds stacked against me. I had roamed through every corner of the city, scanning men's features wherever I went, but my father's face always eluded me.

With the loss of work and apartment and shop, my determination flagged. As my savings dwindled, I needed to find a way to support myself, for I was only forty-one, with plenty of time ahead of me. Through an agency involved with extramural education I found a job as a tutor.

Amity Street was where my first pupil lived. When I initially placed a call to her father, from the other end of the line came a hoarse and hesitant voice. The girl's name was Zheng Xiaomin, her father said; his daughter was a good student, now in fourth grade. He and his wife worked in a factory, for a low income, so it was difficult for them to afford my proposed fifty-yuan-an-hour fee for tutoring their daughter. Hearing a helplessness in his voice that sounded a lot like my own, I suggested he pay me thirty yuan an hour instead, and after a moment he said "Thank you" three times.

We arranged that I would teach the first lesson at four o'clock in the afternoon. I got my hair cut, then went home and had a shave, changed into clean clothes, and put on a cotton overcoat. My overcoat was old, and so were the clothes I wore underneath.

I arrived on Amity Street, in an area I knew well. I knew where up ahead there was a supermarket and where to find Starbucks, McDonald's, and KFC, where there was a street lined with fashion boutiques and where to go for Chinese food.

After I passed these businesses, everything suddenly became unfamiliar. The three six-story apartment buildings that used to overlook Amity Street were now just a heap of ruins. The apartment that I was due to visit for the tutorial session would have been in the second block.

The three buildings had still been standing when I passed this way a few days earlier, with laundry hung out to dry on the balconies and white banners hanging from some of the windows. In big black characters the banners read: "We firmly resist forcible demolition," "We are opposed to violent demolition," and "We will defend our homes to the death."

As I gazed at the ruins, I could dimly make out a few items of clothing caught among the tangle of steel rods and broken concrete. Two excavators and two trucks were stopped nearby, along with a police car in which four policemen sat with the engine running.

A young girl in a red down jacket was sitting alone on a concrete slab, from which severed steel rods jutted out in twisted shapes at both ends. Her satchel was resting on her knees and a textbook and exercise book were lying open on her lap; she was bending down to write something. She had walked out of her own building when she left for school that morning, but it was gone when she came back at the end of the day, and there was no sign of her parents. She sat in the ruins waiting for them to come home, doing her homework and shivering in the cold.

Swaying awkwardly on the debris, I made my way over to where she was. When she raised her head, I saw a face scoured red by the wind.

"Aren't you cold?" I asked.

"Yes, I am," she replied.

I pointed at the KFC nearby. "It'll be warm inside," I said. "Why not do your homework there?"

She shook her head. "My mom and dad wouldn't be able to find me when they come back."

She lowered her head again and went back to doing her homework on the table she had made with her legs. I scanned the ruins.

"Do you know where Zheng Xiaomin lives?" I asked her.

"Right here." She pointed at where she was sitting. "I am Zheng Xiaomin."

Seeing her surprise at my knowing her name, I told her

I was the man engaged to tutor her. She nodded to indicate that she knew of the arrangement, but looked around blankly. "Mom and Dad aren't home yet."

"I'll come back tomorrow," I said.

"We won't be here tomorrow," she said. "Call my dad," she suggested, "he'll know where we'll be tomorrow."

"All right," I said, "I'll call him."

As I clambered back over the rubble, I heard her voice behind me. "Thanks, teacher."

It was the first time I'd been called "teacher." I looked back at the girl in the red down jacket. Sitting there, she softened the ruins.

I walked back to the city square, where now there were gathered two or three thousand people holding banners and shouting slogans—this time it looked as though they really were demonstrating. The perimeter of the square was filled with policemen and police cars, and the police had closed the roads and were preventing others from entering the square. I saw a demonstrator standing on the steps in front of the city government headquarters. He was holding a megaphone and shouting over and over again at the restive crowd: "Keep calm! Please keep calm!"

With the repetition of this message, the demonstrators gradually calmed down. Holding the megaphone in one hand and gesticulating with the other, the man began to address the crowd. "We are here to demand equity and justice. Our demonstration is peaceful. We mustn't do anything extreme, we mustn't give them a pretext to discredit us."

He paused. "I have to inform you all," he continued, "that in the demolitions conducted this morning at Amity Street, a married couple were buried under the rubble and it's not clear if they are alive or dead. . . ."

A van stopped next to me and seven or eight men jumped out of it, their pockets bulging. They went up to the police who were blocking the roads, waved ID in their faces, and then proceeded directly in through the cordon, first with a swaggering confidence, then at a rapid trot. They ran onto the steps in front of the government offices and began to yell, "Smash the city government!"

They pulled stones out of their pockets and threw them at the windows and doors of the city government headquarters; I heard the sound of breaking glass. Police now poured into the square from all directions and began to disperse the crowd; chaos ensued as the demonstrators fled in all directions. Those who tried to resist were soon pinned to the ground. The group of men who had broken the windows came trotting back, nodded to the two policemen standing in front of me, and hopped into the van, which immediately sped off. It had no license plates, I noticed.

That evening I went to a restaurant called Tan Family Eatery. It served tasty food at a reasonable price, and I had become a regular customer, though all I ever ordered was a bowl of noodles. I tried calling Zheng Xiaomin's father several times from the phone next to the cash register, but nobody ever picked up and all I heard was a monotonous ringtone.

On TV they were covering the afternoon's demonstration. The report claimed that a small group of troublemakers had created a disturbance in the square in front of the city government headquarters, misleading those ignorant of the truth and causing damage to public property. The police had detained nineteen suspects and the situation had now been stabilized. The TV did not broadcast any video footage and all we saw were the two news anchors, a man and a woman, reporting this news. Then the media spokesman for the city government—well-dressed, sitting on a sofa—appeared on the screen, taking questions from a network reporter. The reporter would ask a question and the spokesman would answer it, the two of them simply repeating the lines uttered just a few moments earlier by the news anchors. Then the reporter asked if a married couple had been buried in the rubble during the demolitions on Amity Street. The spokesman strenuously denied this, describing it as pure rumor and announcing that those responsible for fabricating it were now in custody. The spokesman finished up by cataloging the outstanding achievements of the city government in recent years and extolling the improvements to people's standard of living.

"Waitress, change the channel!" a man drinking at the table next to me yelled.

A waitress picked up the remote and came over to change the channel. The news spokesman vanished and a soccer game now occupied the screen.

The man turned to me. "Did you hear what those jokers are saying? I don't even believe their punctuation."

I smiled thinly, then bent down again to eat my noodles. During my father's illness, I had brought him here, supporting him by the arm. We sat at a corner table on the ground floor and I ordered his favorite dishes, but he couldn't eat more than a few mouthfuls before throwing it all up. After cleaning up the mess on the table and floor, I had helped him home, saying to the proprietor as we left, "I'm sorry about that."

He gently shook his head. "No worries. Look forward to seeing you next time."

After my father's disappearance, I would come here alone

and sit in that same corner, dolefully eating my noodles. The proprietor would come over and sit opposite me and ask about my father's situation, for he remembered us. On one occasion I broke down and told him my story, how my father had gone off by himself, so that he wouldn't be a burden to me. The proprietor didn't say anything, just looked at me with sympathy.

Later, every time I came here, the proprietor would treat me to a fruit plate at the end of my meal and join me for a chat.

His name was Tan Jiaxin. He and his wife and their daughter and son-in-law ran this restaurant together, with private rooms on the second floor and open seating on the first. They came from Guangdong and sometimes they would bemoan the fact that they had no family ties in this city and no network of connections, so life was hard. Seeing how there was a regular flow of customers and business seemed to be booming, I assumed he was making good money, but he always had a look of worry on his face. Once, he told me that people from public security, emergency services, sanitation, and the commerce and tax bureaus would regularly come and eat extravagant meals, but they refused to pay up front, insisting that everything be put on credit, with some private business or other clearing the debt at the end of the year. At the beginning it wasn't so bad, he said, and seven or eight out of ten of the bills would be paid, but with the economy in poor shape these past few years, many companies had folded and fewer and fewer were coming to settle the accounts, but these government officials still kept coming to feast. So although the restaurant might seem to be doing well, he said, actually the Tans' expenditures exceeded their income. Nobody dares to offend government people, he said.

By the time I finished my noodles, somebody had changed the channel and again there appeared coverage of the afternoon's demonstration. A female reporter was interviewing some people in the street, who all expressed outrage at the reckless behavior of those who had vandalized the government headquarters. Then a professor appeared on the screen, a law professor at the university I had attended. He talked with a slick fluency, first condemning the violence that afternoon, then emphasizing how the people needed to trust and understand and support the government.

Tan Jiaxin brought me a fruit plate. "It's been a while since you were here," he said.

I nodded. But my expression was gloomy and he did not sit down to chat as was his custom. After setting the fruit down on the table, he turned and left.

Slowly I ate the slices of fruit. I also picked up a copy of that day's paper, left behind by another diner. I flipped through the pages until a large photo caught my attention. It was a half-length portrait of an attractive woman; I recognized her at once.

Then I read the accompanying story. Wealthy businesswoman Li Qing had committed suicide the day before by slitting her wrists in her bathtub. She had been implicated in a corruption case involving a highly placed official—the newspaper said she was his mistress, and when people from the investigation bureau went to her home, planning to take her in to help them with their inquiries, they found she had committed suicide. The crowded lines of newsprint filled my gaze like a wall studded with bullet holes. It was a struggle to read the details of the case, for they pained me to the core and I found myself losing the thread of the story.

All of a sudden, thick smoke came billowing out of the

kitchen door. The diners on the ground floor gave cries of alarm and I looked up to see them dashing for the door and running outside. Tan Jiaxin stood at the exit, shouting to the customers to first pay their bill, but several simply pushed him aside and fled. Tan Jiaxin kept shouting and his wife and daughter and son-in-law, joined by several waitresses, ran over to block the exit. They and the customers engaged in a shoving match and there seemed to be a war of words as well. I desperately wanted to read the whole newspaper story, but the uproar in the restaurant just kept getting louder. When I raised my head once more, I saw that the people from the private rooms upstairs were running down the stairs. Reaching the front door, they thrust the Tans aside and bolted in panic into the street. Other customers picked up chairs and smashed windows, then clambered over the windowsills and fled. Before long the waitresses were in full flight too.

I tried my best to ignore the chaos in the dining room and continued to read the newspaper report, but soon the smoke made it impossible to decipher the words on the page. As I rubbed my eyes, people dressed like officials came running down from upstairs and dashed through the dining room, yelling angrily as they approached the front door. After a moment's hesitation, Tan Jiaxin yielded passage to them and they fled out into the street, cursing for all they were worth.

Tan Jiaxin and family remained by the door. He stared at me through the smoke and he seemed to be shouting something. Then there was a deafening roar.

⚫〜∨

I had reached as far as memory's path would lead. No matter how hard I tried to recall what happened next, I could recapture no further moments after this—not even the faintest trace. Tan Jiaxin's stare and the deafening roar that followed it—these were the last scenes that I could find.

In that final scene, my body and soul were transfixed by the news of Li Qing's death, for it awoke in me memories both beautiful and excruciating. My grief for her had been nipped in the bud, long before it had had time to grow to its natural dimensions. Snow was still blowing and the fog showed no sign of dispersing. I continued to wander along the paths of memory. A weariness came over me as I journeyed ever deeper, and I wanted to sit down, so I sat. I don't know whether I sat down on a chair or on a stone, but I seemed to rock back and forth as I sat, like an overladen cargo ship tossed by a swell.

A blind man approached, tapping the hollow ground with his walking stick. When he reached me he came to a stop. "Someone is sitting here," he murmured to himself.

"You're right," I said, "someone *is* sitting here."

He asked me directions to the funeral parlor and I asked him if he had a reservation. He pulled out a ticket, on which was printed A52. I told him he must have taken a wrong turn, for he needed to head back the way he came. He asked me what was written on the paper, and I explained the reservation system at the funeral parlor. He nodded and set off again, and after he had walked into the distance, tapping on the echoless ground, I began to wonder if I had given the blind man the wrong directions, because I myself was lost.

THE SECOND DAY

An unfamiliar female voice was calling my name. "Yang Fei . . ."

The sound seemed to have traveled an immense distance. It lingered as it reached me, then faded like a sigh. I looked around but could not make out from which direction it had come. All I was conscious of was the name winging its way toward me in fragments. "Yang Fei . . . Yang Fei . . ."

It seemed that I had woken up in the place where I had sat down the previous night—a rotting wooden bench. When I sat on it, I had a feeling that it might topple over any moment, and it was a little while before it became as stable as a rock. Rain was falling steadily amid the whirling snow, and oval droplets of water broke open to discharge even more water droplets, some of which continued to fall, some of which disappeared on top of the snow.

A familiar old building emerged vaguely from the rain and snow; in it a one-bedroom apartment had recorded the shapes and sounds of Li Qing and me. I had arrived here in the dark and sat down on a bench as quiet as death, and the fall and flutter of rain and snow were as quiet as death also. Sitting in this silence, I felt on the verge of slumber and closed my eyes once more. That's when I saw the lovely, brilliant Li Qing and our brief love and fleeting marriage. That world was in the process of leaving, and yet the past events in that world were on a bus that was arriving. The scene where I first glimpsed Li Qing slowly approached.

✧

Squeezed in tightly among the standing passengers, I swayed back and forth just as they did. Someone sitting in front of me rose to get off the bus and I moved to take his seat, only to be preempted as a female shape quickly occupied the spot that should have been mine. I was startled by the speed with which the young woman had seized her opportunity, and was equally struck by the beauty of her perfect features. As she raised her head slightly, the eyes of all the men on the bus lingered on her face, but she gave no sign of being aware of that—she seemed to be preoccupied with her own thoughts. It was vexing to me that she had stolen my seat but didn't even give me a look. But I was happy all the same, happy that on a crowded, noisy journey I had the chance to admire her pale skin and delicate profile. After about five stops I started making my way toward the door, which opened as the bus came to a halt. Disembarking passengers squeezed into such a tight mass that I was practically propelled out of the bus. Soon the young woman was skimming past me, as light as a breeze. From behind I watched her dress flutter; she walked and swung her arms with vigor and grace. I followed her into an office block, where she quickly entered an elevator. Its doors closed before I reached it; she was looking out but did not see me.

It turned out that we were working for the same company— it was my first job. As an employee I was unexceptional, but she was already a budding star, with attention-getting beauty and intelligence. The general manager would often take her along with him to business dinners, so she already had considerable experience of the informal negotiations that went on at such events. Women were actually the main topic of conversation at these dinners, with business mentioned only in passing. She discovered that a focus on women helped to bring successful men together: within just a few hours bare acquaintances would become best buddies and cooperation on business deals would proceed smoothly. I heard that at the dinner table she was always poised and chic, adept at putting others at their ease and entertaining men who fancied her, making sure they grinned happily even as she rebuffed them. What's more, she had a formidable capacity for alcohol and could drink most clients under the table. They enjoyed being toasted by Li Qing until they were completely sloshed, and when calling to set up the next banquet they would enjoin our CEO: "Don't forget to bring Li Qing."

The young women in the firm were jealous of her. At midday, in clusters of four or five, they would eat lunch by the window and quietly discuss her endless series of unhappy affairs—communicating a romantic history in which fact and fiction were inextricably mixed. Her love interests—all sons of city officials, apparently—were said to have passed her off as rapidly as a baton in a relay race. Sometimes, as she walked past these young gossips, she'd realize they were circulating rumors about how she had been dumped by these leaders' sons, and she would always send a carefree smile their way, for their gossip and tattle were like scattered raindrops that require no umbrella. Far from having been dumped, she was actually the one who had rejected others' advances, but, proud and aloof, she kept this to herself, because she had no real friends in the company. On the surface she maintained cordial relations with everyone, but in her heart she was a loner.

Suitors pursued her avidly, sending her flowers, giving her presents—sometimes she would be offered several such gifts at the same time, but she would always decline them with a courteous smile. One of our coworkers wouldn't take no for an answer. After trying unsuccessfully for more than a year to induce her to accept his offerings, he ended up declaring his love in the most drastic and dramatic terms. As people were heading off to the elevator at the end of work one day, he knelt down in front of her with a bouquet of roses in hand. Everyone was startled, but soon burst into a round of applause. She turned to him with a smile. "If you kneel down to propose to me," she said, "you'll be on your knees all the time when we're married."

"I'm willing to kneel for you all my life," he answered.

"All right, then," she said. "You kneel here for the rest of your life, and I'll stay single the rest of *my* life."

So saying, she walked around him and into the elevator, and as the doors closed she gazed back toward the office with a smile. If she had noticed me then, she would surely have seen an uneasy expression on my face, for her callousness—or maybe just her composure—made me shiver a little.

The cheers and applause, no longer appropriate, quickly subsided. The kneeling suitor looked around in embarrassment, unsure whether he should stay kneeling or get up right away and make his escape. Much stifled mirth ensued, as women snickered and men looked at each other and chuckled. The onlookers crowded into the elevator and a huge burst of laughter—along with a few coughs—broke out as the doors closed.

When I left the office soon after, the man was still kneeling on the floor, and I wanted to console him but didn't know quite what to say. He wore a wry smile and seemed on the point of making some kind of comment, but ended up saying nothing, simply bowing his head as the flowers lay helplessly on the floor.

Too embarrassed to stay, I entered the empty elevator, and as it made its descent my spirits dropped as well.

The next day the poor man didn't show up for work. The office rang with peals of laughter and everyone was talking about how he knelt to beg for Li Qing's love. Men and women alike said they were burning with curiosity on their morning commute, eager to see if he was still kneeling when they came out of the elevator. His absence was a disappointment, as though life suddenly had lost a lot of its interest. That afternoon he tendered his resignation, arriving in the lobby downstairs and placing a call to one of his coworkers.

"I'm busy right now," the colleague said.

He waved his hands in the air the minute he put the phone down. "He's resigned," he announced loudly. "He doesn't dare come up, so he asked me to collect his things and take them down to him."

After a round of laughter another coworker's phone rang. "I'm in the middle of something," he answered loudly. "How about you come up?"

Laughter again rippled around the office, even before he had time to announce who had called. After a moment of hesitation I stood up and walked over to the suitor's desk. I sorted the things on top of his desk into different categories, then emptied the drawers of their contents, and finally fetched a cardboard box to put all the stuff in. During this time he called a third coworker. "Yang Fei is packing up your things," I heard the colleague say.

When I walked out of the building with the box under my arm, I found the man standing there with an exhausted look on his face. He didn't look me in the eye but simply said "Thank you" as I handed him the box, and then turned and left. As I watched him cross the road with his head down and disappear in the flow of pedestrians, a disconsolate feeling surged up in my heart. He had worked for the company for five years, but in the end his coworkers treated him no differently from a stranger in the street.

After I returned to my desk, a few people came over to inquire what he had said and how he looked. I didn't raise my eyes from my monitor. "He just took the box, that's all," I said.

That day our office—all ten thousand square feet of it—was overflowing with cheerful spirits. I had been working there for a couple of years, and this was the first time I had seen so many people in such a good mood. They recalled the scene of him kneeling on the floor and remembered other ridiculous things he had done in the past, such as how he had once been robbed when walking in a park. Two strangers approached him in broad daylight and asked, "Have you seen any police around?"

"No, I haven't," he said.

"Are you sure?" they pressed him.

"Absolutely," he replied.

That's when they put knives to his throat and demanded his wallet.

The office workers found this story hilarious, and it seemed as though I was the only person who didn't laugh. Later, I just tried to concentrate on my work and made a conscious effort not to listen to their gossip. There were a couple of times when I had to make photocopies and Li

Qing's glance happened to rest on me as I got up. She was sitting diagonally opposite and I turned my head away and didn't look in her direction again. Later, several men went up to her and said ingratiatingly, "No matter what, kneeling at your feet is worth it."

She responded with sarcasm. "You guys want to give it a try too, do you?"

Amid a chorus of laughs, the men had to beat a hasty retreat, saying, "Oh no, we wouldn't dare."

I couldn't help but grin. She had always maintained a cordial tone and this was the first time I had heard her speak so cuttingly. Somehow it made me glad.

Of the young men in the firm, I was probably the only one not to have tried my luck with her, although sometimes I had felt tempted. I knew I was attracted to her, but self-doubt made me rule out any thought I might have a chance with her as sheer impossibility. Our desks were not far apart, but I had never initiated an exchange. I simply drew some satisfaction from her figure and voice being within close proximity. It was a happiness hidden in the heart, a happiness that nobody knew, that she did not know either. She was in public relations and I was in sales, and occasionally she would come over and ask me some work-related question. I would look at her normally and respond in a businesslike fashion. I enjoyed these moments, for then I could appreciate her beauty at ease. After she had dealt so unsparingly with the kneeling suitor, I hesitated to look her in the eye. But still she would come over and ask me things about work, and she did so more frequently. Every time, I would answer with lowered eyes.

A few days after the incident, I left work a bit later than usual. When the elevator doors opened, she was standing in the elevator by herself, having descended from the executive floor. As I hesitated about whether to join her, she pressed the open-door button. "In you come," she said.

I got on. It was the first time I had been alone with her. "How's he doing?" she asked.

I was startled for a moment, before I realized she meant the man who had proposed to her on bended knee. "He looked tired," I said. "Maybe he spent the whole night walking the streets."

I heard a sharp intake of breath. "It really made me look bad, the way he behaved."

"He made himself look bad too," I said. I watched the numbers of the floors flashing by as the elevator descended.

"Do you think me a bit callous?" she asked abruptly.

I did think that, but what struck me more was the forlorn tone in her voice. "I think you're lonely," I said. "You don't seem to have any friends."

Somehow my eyes were wet. I had never thought about her outside work hours, because I had always told myself that I was not even on her radar, but at that moment I suddenly was sad for her. I felt a tap on my arm, and looked down to find her proffering a mini-pack of tissues. I took one and gave her the rest back.

In the days that followed, we carried on as before, each of us arriving at work and leaving work at our own time, and with her often coming over to ask me things. I continued to look at her in a routine way as I answered her queries. Apart from this we had no other interaction. Although her eyes would light up when she saw me in the morning, our little encounter in the elevator didn't make me start getting ideas—I just felt we had formed more of a connection. I was content that I could see her at work and had no inkling that she had developed feelings for me.

In those days the most glorious thing for a girl was to marry the son of an official, but Li Qing was an exception, for she could see at a glance that those spoiled young bucks would not make good lifetime companions. At the business dinners that she attended along with the general manager, she observed the ingratiating manners of many successful men who pursued other women behind the backs of their wives, and it may have been that experience that determined her criterion for selecting a mate, causing her to seek a loyal, dependable man—someone like me.

My emotional state then was cramped and confined, like a room with tightly sealed windows and doors: although love's footsteps could be heard outside the room, I felt they were steps heading somewhere else—until one day when the steps came to a halt and the bell rang.

It was a late afternoon in spring. The office was empty of people, for I was working overtime to finish an assignment. I heard the sound of high heels tapping on the marble floor and coming closer. When I raised my head, there she was with a smile on her face. "You know what?" she said. "Last night I dreamt we were married."

I was dumbfounded. How could that possibly happen?

She looked at me. "Funny, isn't it?" she mused.

So saying, she turned around and walked away. The sound of her high heels hitting the floor was as loud as my heartbeat; even after the sound faded away, my heart continued to pound.

I began to fantasize, and in the following days my mind would easily wander. Late at night, again and again I would think back to her look and her tone when she mentioned the dream, and I would speculate cautiously about whether or not she was interested in me. With her on my mind so much, one night I too dreamt that she and I were married—

not in a bustling wedding scene but with the two of us holding hands as we went to the local registry office to fill in the
forms. When I saw her at the office the next day, I suddenly
blushed. She was quick to notice, and when nobody else was
around, she asked me, with a searching look, "Why do you
blush when you see me?"

"Last night I dreamt that you and I went to the registry
office," I said timidly.

She beamed. "Meet me outside after work," she said softly.

What a long day that was—almost as long, it seemed, as
the years of my youth. I kept losing focus, giving distracted
answers to my coworkers' questions. The hands of the clock
moved with unbearable slowness, and at times even breathing seemed a strain. Finally, through sheer willpower, I made
it to the end of the workday, but when I stood on the street
outside, I still found breathing an effort, not knowing whether
she was having to work overtime or was deliberately dragging
her feet in order to test my devotion. It wasn't until dark that
I saw her appear. She paused briefly on the steps, looked
around in all directions, and after seeing me she ran down
the steps. Dodging the cars going back and forth, she crossed
the road and ran up to me, smiling. "Are you hungry? This is
going to be my treat."

She took my arm and marched forward briskly, as though
we were longtime lovers instead of on our first date. I was
startled, then immediately bathed in happiness.

In the days that followed, I often wondered if this was
really happening. We arranged to meet every morning at
a bus stop and take the bus together to the office. I would
arrive at the stop at least an hour before the appointed time
and get nervous that she wouldn't show up; I wouldn't feel
at ease until I saw her elegant figure loping toward me, her
arms swinging by her sides. That's when I knew it was real.

Together we arrived at work and together we left, and even after ten days of this nobody had realized that we were dating, probably assuming—as I had earlier—that for us to get together was unthinkable. Sometimes, at the end of the day, I would have finished my work and she would have more to do, so I'd sit at my desk waiting for her.

"How come you're still here?" a coworker asked.

"I'm waiting for Li Qing," I replied.

A strange smile appeared on his face, as though he was amused to see me falling into the old familiar trap.

At other times she would finish first and I would have more work still to do, in which case she'd sit down next to me.

When coworkers passed, they would have a different expression on their faces, and they'd ask her in astonishment, "How come you're still here?"

"I'm waiting for him," she would reply.

News of our romance spread like wildfire. The men found it baffling: in their eyes, Li Qing falling for me after rejecting the sons of city officials was like someone favoring a sesame seed over a watermelon. Thinking themselves in no way inferior to me, they smarted with the injustice and muttered to each other that "it's true that 'the fresh flower gets stuck in a cowpat' and 'the scabby toad gets to eat swan meat.'" The women, for their part, rejoiced at Li Qing's lapse of judgment: on seeing me they would smile meaningfully and draw a lesson from what had happened. "No need to set your sights too high when looking for a mate—more-or-less is good enough. Just look at Li Qing there—she spends all that time playing the field and ends up with a loser."

For the two of us, immersed in our love, these comments were—in Li Qing's words—just "grass blowing in the wind." But she had quite a temper, and when she found I was being written off as a cowpat, a scabby toad, and a loser, she resorted to coarse language and said they were talking through their asses.

"You're handsome," she said, gazing into my face.

"I'm a loser, it's true," I admitted.

"No," she said. "You are good. You are loyal. You are reliable."

We walked hand in hand along the evening streets and sat for a long time on a bench in a quiet part of the park. Tired, she leaned her head on my shoulder and I put my arm around her—that was when we kissed for the first time. Later, when we sat in her apartment, she revealed her tender side, detailing the ordeal of accompanying the CEO to business banquets, the lustful glances and indecent language of those high-flyers, how she loathed them but still had to flatter them with a smile and down shots in their honor, then go to the bathroom to throw up, after which she continued to toast them. That she dated the sons of city officials was all just rumor—she had only met three such young men, introduced to her by the boss, and each of them displayed his own version of the playboy style: the first was full of himself, the second spent all his time ogling her, while the third started feeling her up the first chance he got. When she resisted, smiling apologetically, he said, "Don't give me that act." Her parents lived in another province, and after such humiliations she would call them up in a tearful mood, but then force herself to be cheerful, telling them that everything was fine and not to worry.

Her story made me feel sad. I took her face in my hands and kissed her eyes, tickling her until she smiled. She said she had noticed me from early on and realized that I was a hard worker, observing too that when an office slacker claimed credit for my achievements, I never made an issue of this. I told her there were times when I was really angry and wanted to give him a piece of my mind, but I found I just couldn't get the words out.

"Sometimes I hate how weak I am," I told her.

"You won't get tough with me, will you?" she said, caressing my face affectionately.

"Certainly not," I said.

When the other young men in the company pursued her in their various fashions, she told me, I seemed to remain completely cold. That's what got her curious and that's why she came over to ask questions and study my reaction; she found that I gave her a simple, friendly glance quite different from the way her other male coworkers looked at her. Later, that incident of the suitor declaring his love on his knees left her with a positive impression, for she quietly observed how amid the laughter I collected the man's possessions and delivered them to him. She paused for a moment, and then said that the more favor she enjoyed in the business world, the more lonesome she felt when she returned at night to her rented room—that was when she really wanted to be with someone she loved. When we happened to meet in the elevator and my eyes got wet, she suddenly felt the warmth of another person's concern, and in the days that followed she became more and more convinced that I was the right man for her.

Then she pinched my nose. "Why didn't *you* pursue me?"

"I just lack ambition," I said.

We married a year later. My father's dorm unit was too small to accommodate all three of us, so we rented a one-bedroom apartment as our new home. My father was overjoyed that I was marrying such an able and attractive wife.

And Li Qing was good to him: on weekends, when he stayed overnight with us, we would both go meet him, and after we all crowded onto the bus she could always somehow find him a seat. This reminded me of the first time I saw her, and I would smile at the thought. During Spring Festival we took the train to see her parents, who worked at a state-owned factory. Kind and down-to-earth, they were happy that their daughter had married a solid, dependable man.

Our married life was calm and happy. She continued to escort the boss to business dinners, however. After dark I would wait at home alone and often she would get back very late and very tired. I would smell alcohol on her breath when I hugged her, and she would rest her head on my chest for a bit before we went to bed. She hated these boisterous banquets but found it impossible to decline such invitations, for by this time she was the deputy head of public relations. She didn't care for this position, which in her words amounted pretty much to "deputy head of swigging and swilling." "Beauty is a woman's travel permit," she once said to me. But she was using the permit for the company's benefit, never for herself.

After a couple of years we began planning the purchase of an apartment of our own, and at the same time decided it was time to have a child—she thought that then she would have a compelling reason to turn down those tiresome engagements. So she stopped using contraception. It was precisely at this point, however, that events took a different course. A chance encounter on a business trip drove home to her the difference between us: she was the kind of person who could shape her own destiny, whereas I could only be carried along by my own fate.

The person sitting next to her on the plane was a Ph.D.,

recently returned from the United States. Ten years older than she, with a wife and child, he had just started up his own business, and during their two-hour flight he spoke with passion about his glowing prospects. I think it must have been her looks that first attracted him, inspiring him to wax so eloquent and say so much, and having attended so many functions with our CEO she was well-positioned to give him helpful advice. Enchanted by her beauty, he must have soon been impressed by her acuteness of observation and attention to detail, and so he issued an invitation right there on the plane: "Why don't you join me?"

When they reached their destination, he didn't stay at the hotel that he had booked but moved to the one where she was staying, to show how much he valued her advice. That's what he said, at least, but I suspect it was something else he was after. During the day they worked separately at their jobs and in the evenings they sat down at the hotel bar to discuss the challenges of entrepreneurship. She was full of ideas. Not only did she brainstorm new business strategies, she also briefed him on the subtle arts of getting things done in China, like how to cozy up to government officials and supply them with perks. After all those years in America, he was a bit out of touch with the unspoken rules that govern Chinese realities. When the two went their separate ways, he again expressed his interest in working with her. She smiled and did not answer, but gave him her home phone number.

In her heart, a change was taking place. To our CEO, she had good looks and a good head on her shoulders, but he never realized the full extent of her talent and ambition. Now, at last, she felt she had found someone who could truly understand her.

After she got home, she resumed her use of contraception, saying it was too soon to have a child. Then every evening he would call and she would talk to him on the phone, sometimes for an hour, sometimes twice that. At the beginning it was often I who answered the calls, but later I stopped picking up when the phone rang. Initially, it was all about business: he asked her questions, she pondered for a minute, then answered him. Later, she would just hold the phone and listen to him talk, saying very little herself. After hanging up she would fall into deep thought, and it would be a while before she realized that I was sitting there and forced a smile. I could tell that their topic had moved on. I said nothing, but my heart was racked with pain.

Six months later he arrived in our city, by which time he had already finalized his divorce. After dinner that day she told me she was going round to his hotel. I sat on the sofa the whole evening, my mind completely blank, as though I'd lost the capacity for thought. She didn't return until dawn. Expecting me to be asleep, she opened the door carefully, only to find me sitting on the sofa. She gave a start, then came over timidly and sat down next to me.

She had always been such a confident woman, and this was the first time I had seen her so ill at ease. Her head bowed, she told me shakily that the man had got divorced for her sake. She felt she belonged with him—they were such an ideal match. I said nothing. He had divorced his wife for her, she repeated. I noticed the emphatic tone in her voice and I thought: Any man would be willing to get divorced for your sake. But I said nothing, knowing I had lost her. With me she would only have a humdrum, uneventful life, whereas with him she could build up a whole business. In fact, six months earlier I had already had the faint awareness that she would leave me, and this sensation had only grown stronger during the intervening time. Now that premonition had become fact.

She gave a deep sigh. "Let's get a divorce."

"All right," I said.

After saying this, I couldn't help shedding a few tears. Although I didn't want us to break up, there was nothing I could do to make her stay. She raised her head and saw me crying, and she wept too. She wiped her tears away with her hand, saying, "I'm sorry, I'm sorry . . ."

I rubbed my eyes. "Don't say sorry," I said.

That morning the two of us went to the office together as usual. I requested a day's leave and she handed in her notice, then we went to the neighborhood registry office to attend to the divorce paperwork. While she went home to pack her bags, I went to the bank and withdrew all our savings, which came to sixty thousand yuan—the money we had set aside to purchase an apartment. Once I got home, I handed her all the cash. She hesitated a moment, then took twenty thousand. I shook my head and urged her to take the full amount. Twenty thousand was enough, she insisted. That'll make me worry, I said. She bowed her head and said I didn't need to worry, I should know how capable she was; she could handle everything perfectly well. She put twenty thousand yuan in her bag and left the rest on the table. Then she gazed fondly at the home we had shared. "I should go now," she said.

I helped her collect her clothes and other belongings, which we stuffed into two large suitcases, and I carried the cases down to the street below. She was going first to his hotel and then the two of them would go to the airport, so I hailed a cab and put her cases in the trunk. The moment of parting had now arrived. I waved goodbye to her, but she came forward and hugged me tightly. "I still love you," she said.

"I'll always love you," I replied.

She started crying. "I'll write you and call you," she said.

"Don't write and don't call," I said. "That will just upset me."

She got into the cab and as it pulled away she didn't look at me but brushed away her tears. That's how she left, heading off on the path of life that fate had chosen for her.

For my father, my sudden divorce was a bolt out of the blue. He looked at me with a face of pure shock as I briefly explained the reasons for the divorce. I said that our marriage was a misunderstanding from the start, because I was simply not good enough for her. He just kept shaking his head, unable to accept what I was saying. "All along I thought she was a good girl," he lamented. "I misjudged her."

My father's coworkers Hao Qiangsheng and Li Yuezhen, a married couple, were equally shocked when they heard the news. Qiangsheng insisted categorically that the man was a confidence trickster and would dump Li Qing without batting an eye. In his view, she didn't know what was good for her and would be sure to end up regretting her decision. Yuezhen had always been fond of Li Qing, saying she was smart and pretty and understanding. But now Yuezhen was convinced Li Qing was a gold digger, and she bemoaned the fact that there were more and more such women in this society where you get more respect if you're a whore than if you're poor. Yuezhen tried to comfort me, saying there was no shortage of young women better than her—she knew a good half dozen. She introduced me to several, sure enough, but none of these possibilities went anywhere. I take most of the responsibility for that: in our time together Li Qing had gradually and imperceptibly reshaped my expectations, until she achieved a peerless position in my mind. On dates with those other girls, I couldn't help but compare them to her and always ended up disappointed.

In the months and years that followed, I sometimes saw her interviewed on television or read stories about her in newspapers and magazines. She seemed to me both familiar and foreign: familiar in her smile and demeanor, foreign in the content and tone of her conversation. I got the feeling that she was the prime mover in the company's operations and her husband was just playing a supporting role. I was happy for her, for on TV and in the press she was as pretty as ever, and she was using that travel permit for herself at last. But then I was sad for myself, for our time together had just been a detour in her life and only after leaving me did she get on the true path.

In the hollow silence I heard once more the call of that unfamiliar woman's voice: "Yang Fei . . ."

I opened my eyes and looked all around. The rain-snow mix was now falling less heavily. To my left there approached a woman very much like Li Qing, wearing a nightdress that was dripping with water. She came up to me and studied my face and then my pajamas, on which she saw the now-faded characters for "Li Qing." "Yang Fei?" she called inquiringly.

She had to be Li Qing, I felt. But why did her voice sound so different? I sat on the bench looking at her silently.

A strange expression appeared on her face. "You're wearing Yang Fei's pajamas," she said. "Who are you?"

"I'm Yang Fei," I said.

She looked at my peculiar features in perplexity. "You don't look like Yang Fei to me."

I put my hand to my face. My left eye was on my cheek and my nose next to my nose and my chin below my chin.

"I forgot to get my face fixed," I said.

She reached out her hands and carefully put my eyeball back inside its socket and moved my askew nose back to its original position and pushed my wandering chin up with a firm click.

Then she took a step back and studied me carefully. "Now you look like Yang Fei," she said.

"I *am* Yang Fei," I said. "You look like Li Qing."

"I *am* Li Qing."

We both smiled, and in smiling our familiar smiles we recognized each other.

"You're Li Qing," I said.

"You really are Yang Fei," she said.

"Your voice is different."

"So is yours."

We looked at each other.

"Your voice is like that of someone I don't know," I said.

"Your voice is like that of a stranger," she said.

"It's so strange," I said. "I know your voice so well, and even your breathing."

"It seems strange to me," she replied. "I ought to be familiar with your voice. . . ." She paused and then smiled. "Just like I'm familiar with your snore."

Her body leaned over and her hand patted my pajama top, patted my collar. "The collar is still in good shape," she said.

"I never wore these after you left," I said.

"So how come you're wearing them now?"

"They will serve as a shroud."

"Shroud?" She didn't really understand.

"How about your pajamas?" I asked.

"I didn't wear them, either," she said. "I don't know where I put them."

"You were right not to wear them," I said. "They've got my name on them."

"That's true," she said. "I married someone else."

I nodded.

"I kind of regret it." A mischievous smile appeared on her face. "I should have worn them, just to see what his reaction would be."

Then she became sad. "Yang Fei, I've come to say goodbye."

I saw how water droplets were still trailing from her nightgown. "Were you wearing that when you lay down in the bathtub?" I asked.

Her eyes glinted, in an expression I knew well. "You know what happened, do you?" she asked.

"I know."

"When did you hear about it?"

"Yesterday"—I thought for a moment—"or maybe the day before."

She studied me carefully and seemed to realize something. "You died too?"

"Yes," I said. "I did."

We exchanged mournful looks.

"It looks like you're grieving for me," she said.

"I have the same feeling about you," I said. "It's as though we're both grieving for each other."

She looked around in perplexity. "Where are we?"

I pointed at the old building that appeared dimly behind the rain and snow. She gazed at it intently, recalling the apartment that had once recorded the humdrum minutiae of our life.

"Do you still live there?" she asked.

I shook my head. "I moved out after you left."

"You moved in with your dad?"

I nodded.

"Now I know why I came here." She smiled.

"It must have been in our destiny," I agreed. "We both had to make our way back here."

"Who lives in the apartment now?"

"I don't know."

She shifted her gaze, clutching her wet gown tightly to her chest. "I'm tired—I walked a long way to get here."

"I didn't walk far," I said, "but I feel tired too."

Her body bent over once again, and she started to sit down on the bench, to my left. She felt it sway precariously. "This bench seems about to collapse," she said.

"You'll get used to it in a minute," I said.

She sat down gingerly and her body tensed up. But after a moment her body relaxed. "It won't collapse anymore," she said.

"It feels like sitting on a rock," I said.

"That's right," she agreed.

We sat quietly together as though sitting in a dream. A lot of time seemed to pass before her voice regained its strength.

"How did you get here?" she asked.

"I don't know." I thought of the last scene I remembered. "I was in a restaurant and had just finished eating a bowl of noodles. The newspaper on the table carried a story about you. The kitchen seemed to catch on fire and many people fled outside. I didn't move but just kept on reading the story in the paper. Then there was an explosion and I don't know what happened after that."

"This happened yesterday?" she asked.

"It might have been the day before," I said.

"It was all my fault."

"Not your fault," I said, "the newspaper's."

She leaned her head on my shoulder. "Do you mind if I lean on your shoulder?"

"You're already doing that," I said.

She seemed to smile and her head trembled a couple of times on my shoulder. She saw the black armband on my left arm and reached out a hand to touch it.

"Are you wearing this for me?" she asked.

"For myself."

"Nobody is wearing black for you?"

"No."

"How about your dad?"

"He died, over a year ago now. He was very ill and knew there was no cure, and so as not to burden me he went off quietly by himself. I looked for him everywhere but couldn't find him."

"He was an excellent father, and very kind to me as well."

"The best father there could be," I said.

"How about your wife?"

I didn't answer.

"Do you have a child?"

"No, I don't. I never married again."

"Why not?"

"I wasn't interested."

"Was it because you were so hurt?"

"No," I said. "It was because I never met another woman like you."

"I'm sorry." All this time she had been gently patting my black armband.

"Do you have a child?" I asked.

"For a while I did want one," she said, "but later I gave up on the idea."

"Why was that?"

"I got an STD—picked up from him."

I felt droplets in the corners of my eyes, droplets different from rain and snow, and I stretched out my right hand to wipe away these drops.

"Are you crying?" she asked.

"I guess I am," I said.

"Crying for me?"

"Probably that's what it is."

"He kept a mistress outside and also went to clubs to pick up women, and I split up with him after I got infected." She sighed. "Do you know something? I would think of you at night."

"After you broke up?"

"That's right." She hesitated. "After being with someone."

"You fell in love with another man?"

"I didn't love him," she said. "He was an official. After doing it with him, I would think of you."

I smiled ruefully.

"Are you jealous?"

"It's a long time since we were married."

"Each time he left, I would lie in bed thinking of you. When we were together," she said softly, "I had to do a lot of entertaining. You would never go to sleep, however late it was, but would stay up waiting for me. I would be exhausted when I got home and just want you to hold me in your arms. It was when I leaned on you that I could relax at last. . . ."

Water droplets again appeared in the corners of my eyes and my right hand again wiped them away.

"Did you miss me?" she asked.

"I was constantly trying to forget you."

"Did you succeed?"

"Not completely."

"I knew you wouldn't forget me," she said. "He probably has."

"Where is he now?" I asked.

"He went to Australia," she said. "As soon as he heard rumors they were going to audit our company, he upped and ran—without telling me."

I shook my head. "He didn't act much like a husband."

She smiled thinly. "I married twice, but only had one husband—and that was you."

Once again my right hand went up to rub my eyes.

"Are you crying again?" she asked.

"It's because I'm happy," I said.

She spoke of her final moments. "I lay in the tub and heard the people who had come to arrest me kicking the front door and shouting my name, like bandits. I watched as clouds of blood swam about in the water like fish, slowly expanding until the water became redder and redder. . . . Do you know something? I was thinking of you the whole time, thinking of that little apartment where we lived."

"So that's how you come to be here."

"That's right," she said. "It's been a long trip."

She raised her head from my shoulder. "Were you still living at your dad's place?"

"We sold the apartment so we could afford to pay for his treatment."

"So where are you now?"

"In a cheap rental."

"Take me to see it."

"It's very small and run-down—dirty too."

"I don't mind."

"I would feel uncomfortable."

"I'm very tired. I'd like to lie down on a bed."

"All right."

We both stood up. The rain and snow, scanty just a few minutes earlier, were now once more densely filling the air. Then she took my arm and it was as though our love affair was rekindled. We walked close together along a vague road, for I don't know how long, until we came to my rental. As I opened the door, she saw the two notices demanding I pay the electricity and water bills and I heard her sigh.

"Why do you sigh?" I asked.

"You still owe money."

I ripped the notes down. "I already paid these bills."

We entered my untidy little apartment. She seemed not to notice the chaos and lay down on the bed while I sat on a chair nearby. After she lay down her gown opened—it must have been just as exhausted as she was. She closed her eyes and her body seemed to float on the bed. After a moment her eyes opened.

"Why are you sitting there?" she asked.

"I'm looking at you."

"Come and lie next to me."

"I'm fine just sitting."

"Come."

"No, I'll just stay where I am."

"Why?"

"I'd be a bit embarrassed."

She sat up and reached a hand out toward me. I gave her my hand and she pulled me onto the bed. We lay there shoulder to shoulder, our hands clasped, and I heard her even breathing, like little ripples spreading across a calm lake. After a while she talked softly and I too began to talk. Once again I was gripped by an odd sensation: I knew that I was in bed with a familiar woman, but her unfamiliar voice gave me the feeling that I was lying with someone I had never met before. I shared this feeling I had with her and she said she felt the same way, that she was lying with a strange man.

"How about this?" She turned toward me. "Let's face each other." I turned toward her. "Does that feel better now?" she asked.

"Yes," I said.

Her wet hand stroked my damaged face. "The day we broke up," she said, "when you saw me into the taxi, I hugged you and said something to you—do you remember?"

"Yes, I remember," I said. "You said you still loved me."

"That's right." She nodded. "You said something to me too."

"I said I'd always love you."

She and the gown together climbed on top of me and I didn't know quite what to do. I raised my hands but didn't dare hug her. Her mouth said wetly into my ear: "My STD is cured."

"That's not what I meant."

"Hug me."

I hugged her.

"Caress me."

My hands caressed her back, waist, and thighs—I caressed her everywhere. Her body was wet and my hands seemed to be caressing her in water.

"You've put on some weight," I said.

She smiled faintly. "I've gotten a little thicker around the waist."

My hands caressed her restlessly, and then it was my body caressing her body while her body caressed my body and it was as though our bodies developed cords that connected us. . . .

I sat up in bed and saw her standing by the bed, tidying her hair with her hand.

"You woke up."

"I never slept."

"I heard you snoring."

"I really didn't sleep."

"All right," she said. "You didn't."

She fastened her belt. "I've got to go. Friends have prepared a big funeral for me, so I need to hurry back."

I nodded.

She walked over to the door and looked back at me as she left. "Yang Fei, I'm off now," she said disconsolately.

THE THIRD DAY

I roamed on the borderline between life and death. The snow was bright and the rain was dark. I seemed to be walking in morning and evening, both at the same time.

More than once I walked toward my bedsit. Yesterday Li Qing and I had left traces there of our reunion, but today there was no way to get close to it. However much I walked, I seemed to be stationary and never got the least bit nearer to my building. I remembered how I had taken my father's hand when I was small, thinking to walk until we stood right underneath the moon, but, though we walked a long way, the distance between us and the moon did not change in the slightest.

Just at this moment two shining rails grew up beneath my feet and swirled ahead of me. They appeared tentatively, like rays of light that had lost their way, but they led me to the scene of my birth.

I was delivered between two rails as a train sped off in the night, and I gave my earliest wail not amid howling wind and pounding rain, but under a sky full of stars. A young switch-man heard my feeble sobs and came to rescue me, while another train made the adjacent track quiver as it rushed toward me from the far distance. No sooner did the switchman clutch me to his chest than that train raced past with a deafening roar, and that is how, between the time it took for the first train to go one way and the second train to go the other, I acquired a father. A few days later, I had acquired a name as well—Yang Fei. This father of mine was called Yang Jinbiao.

I entered the world through the strangest of channels, for my delivery was effected not in a hospital's obstetric unit or at my mother's home, but in the cramped toilet of a train in motion.

Forty-one years ago, my birth mother boarded a train in the ninth month of a pregnancy. I was to be her third child, and she was heading back to her parental home to visit my ailing grandmother. As the train slowly approached a station ten hours into its journey, she felt a faint ache in her midriff. I was still three weeks away from my scheduled first appearance, and my older brother and sister had both been born strictly in keeping with the usual timetable, so my mother assumed I would follow a similar course. She simply felt that she needed to go to the toilet, and had no inkling that I was impatient to come out.

She rose from her sleeping berth and waddled down the aisle toward the toilet at the end of the railroad car. The train had just pulled into a station, and her passage to the toilet was made all the more difficult by the travelers who had crammed their way onto the train with bags over their shoulders. She carefully squeezed her way past the passengers and their big and small bags. As she entered the toilet, the train slowly began to move. Trains in those days had primitive facilities and squat-toilets only; if you looked down through the spacious round hole you saw an endless succession of railroad sleepers flash past below. With me in her belly hampering her movements, my mother was unable to squat down and had to kneel, trying to ignore the filth on the toilet floor. Pulling down her pants, she gave an effort and out I popped—and down into the round hole in the toilet floor. It took only a second for the speed of my slide and the speed of the train's forward motion to break the cord that linked me to my mother, and immediately we were lost to each other.

My mother lay slumped on the floor in acute pain; it took a few moments for her to realize that her womb was now empty. After looking around for me in panic, she realized that I must have fallen out through the hole. With great effort she managed to prop herself up, and after opening the toilet door she cried out to a passenger waiting outside, "My baby, my baby—"

With that she collapsed in a heap, and there was a shout of "Somebody has fainted!"

First a female attendant rushed up, and then the conductor. The female attendant was the first to see blood between my mother's legs, and she prompted the conductor to broadcast an appeal for medical personnel to proceed at once to carriage 11. Two doctors and a nurse rushed to the scene, to find my mother lying sprawled in the passageway, sobbing and begging for help in incoherent fragments of speech. Soon she fainted again and had to be lifted onto her sleeping berth. The three medical workers attended to her while the train trundled on.

By this time I was already in the cabin where the switchman lived. This young man—at twenty-one, now suddenly a father—looked at me in consternation. I was covered in purple-red blotches and crying fit to burst, my umbilical cord quivering in time with my crying and making him wonder if I had grown a tail. As my sobs grew weaker, it dawned on him that I must be hungry. It was late at night then and all the shops were shut, so he could find no infant formula for me. In his anxiety he remembered that the wife of a coworker of his named Hao Qiangsheng had given birth to a daughter three days earlier, so he wrapped me up in his cotton-padded overcoat and dashed toward Hao's apartment.

Hao Qiangsheng was woken from sleep by a pounding on his door, and, opening up, he saw Yang was carrying something in his arms and crying desperately, "Milk! Milk!"

Still not fully awake, Hao rubbed his eyes. "What milk?" he asked.

Yang opened his coat to show him the wailing infant inside, then immediately passed me on to our host. Hao gave a start, accepting me as gingerly as he might a piping-hot roast sweet potato, and with a face of utter amazement carried me into the inner room. "It's Yang Jinbiao's," he said to his wife, Li Yuezhen, who had also just woken up. From one look at me Li Yuezhen could tell that I was newborn, so she took me into her arms, and after she pulled up her shirt I quieted down and began to gulp down my first milk.

Yang sat with Hao in the outer room, mopping his brow, and explained what had happened. Only now did Hao get the full picture. He told my father how flabbergasted he had been to see he had suddenly acquired a child, when he didn't even have a girlfriend. My father chuckled loudly at this, but soon shared with Hao his concern that I might be a freak, given that I had a tail—and one attached to the front of me.

Inside, Li Yuezhen overheard this exchange between the two new fathers, and after I had drunk my fill and dropped off to sleep she dressed me in a set of her daughter's home-made baby clothes and went into the outer room with a wad of used fabric in her hand.

Li Yuezhen returned me to my father's arms and instructed him on how to change diapers, showing him how to cut up old clothes to make diapers—the older the clothes the better, because the older the softer. Finally she pointed at the thing protruding from my navel. "That's the umbilical cord," she said. "Tomorrow you need to go to the station clinic and have the doctor cut it off. Don't try to do it yourself—the baby might pick up an infection."

I walked on, following the rails that looked like light beams, looking for that rickety cabin next to the railroad line that harbored so many stories from my early years. In front of me was rain and snow, and in front of the rain and snow were row upon row of tall buildings dotted with dark windows. They retreated as I walked toward them, and I realized that that world was gradually leaving me.

Faintly I could hear the sound of my father lamenting the ways of the world, a sound so far away and yet so intimate. In my ears his complaints began to stack up high, just like those tall buildings in the far distance, and they brought a smile to my lips.

For a long time Yang Jinbiao was convinced that my birth parents must have abandoned me on the railroad tracks because they intended me to be run over by a train, and for this reason he would often mutter to himself, "I could never have imagined there could be such heartless parents on this earth."

This stubborn conviction made him all the more devoted to me. From the time he plucked me up from between the rails, I was never out of his sight. At the beginning, I spent my days in a cotton sling. The first such sling was made by Li Yuezhen, out of blue cotton; the later ones, also blue, were made by my adoptive father himself. Every day when he left home to go to work, he would mix milk formula and pour it into a bottle, then stuff the bottle into his clothes, next to his beating heart, so that his own body heat could keep the bottle warm. Then he would lower me into the sling around his neck. Hanging by his side was an army-issue canteen, and on his back he carried two bundles, one stuffed full of clean diapers, the other one empty, ready to be stuffed with my dirty diapers.

He would walk back and forth when he had to change the switches at forks in the railroad line, and I would sway back and forth on his chest. Surely there could be no finer cradle, and the sleep I had as a baby was the sweetest I ever had. If it hadn't been for hunger, I think I might never have woken up when in my father's arms. When I burst out bawling, my father would know I was hungry and would feel for the bottle, then stuff the nipple into my mouth. I grew up day by day sucking on the bottle, in my father's body heat. Later, when I woke up hungry, I no longer bawled but stretched out a hand to feel for the bottle. That action delighted him no end, and he ran to tell Hao Qiangsheng and Li Yuezhen how smart I was.

My father soon attuned himself perfectly to my needs, knowing when I was hungry and when I was thirsty. When I was thirsty, he would take a mouthful of water from his canteen and then slowly transfer it from his mouth to mine. He was able to distinguish—or so he told Li Yuezhen—the subtle difference between the sound I made when I was hungry and the sound I made when I was thirsty. Li Yuezhen wasn't sure whether to believe him, for she depended on the time of day to determine whether her daughter was hungry or whether she was thirsty.

If my father caught a whiff of something smelly as he tramped along the railroad line, he knew he needed to change my diaper. He would squat down next to the tracks, lay me on the ground, and as trains trundled by he would wipe my bottom with grass paper and fasten a clean diaper around me. Then with a lump of soil he would briskly wipe away most of the mess on my diapers, and then fold them up and place them in the other bag. After he got home at the end of the day, he would set me down on the bed and use soap and running water to wash the dirty diapers.

Our home was a little cabin some twenty yards from the railroad tracks. Outside the door, diapers were hung out to dry at various heights, like leaves hanging from a tree.

I grew up amid the sounds of trains rumbling by, in the shaking and trembling little house. When I was a bit bigger, the cotton sling on my father's chest gave way to a cotton sling on his back, and that sling slowly got bigger too as I continued to grow.

My father had quick hands, and he soon taught himself how to tailor clothes and knit sweaters. During work hours, his coworkers couldn't help laughing when they saw him, because he would knit a little sweater for me as he walked along the tracks, with fingerwork so expert that he didn't need to look at what he was doing.

After I learned to walk, we would hold hands. On weekends my father would take me to the park to play. There, confident in the safety of our surroundings, he would let go of my hand and follow along behind as I ran around everywhere. We were very much attuned to each other's needs, and if we were going down a little path I would sense at once, even without looking, when my father stretched out his arm, and would give him my little hand right away.

After we returned to the house next to the tracks, my father would be vigilant in protecting me from dangers, and when he was cooking inside and I wanted to play outside, he would attach us with a cord, one end tied to his foot and one end tied to mine, so that I grew up within the safety zone that he had defined. I could roam around near our front door, but if I saw a train approaching and couldn't resist going closer to the tracks, I would hear the warning shout of my father from within the room: "Yang Fei, come back!"

The little house that I had been looking for appeared, just as the two rails were drifting off into the distance. A second earlier it had not been there, but the next second it was. I saw myself as a young child and my father as a young man, and also a young woman with her hair tied in a long braid. The three of us emerged from the house. My face looked vaguely familiar, my father's face I remembered as though it were yesterday, but the girl's face was indistinct.

As a little boy I was happy as a lark, utterly unaware that I was ruining my father's life. My railside birth had narrowed his path dramatically. He had no girlfriend, and marriage was now only the remotest possibility. His best friends, Hao Qiangsheng and Li Yuezhen, introduced him to several prospects, informing them ahead of time about my foundling origins, so as to make clear that my father was a kindhearted and reliable man. But when those young women met him for the first time, if he wasn't changing my diapers he'd be knitting a sweater for me, and the sight of him in full domestic mode, although making them smile, would also make them turn around and leave.

It was when I was four that I met the young woman with her hair in a braid. She was three years older than my father. She had missed the scenes of diaper changing and sweater knitting and saw simply a rather cute little boy. She reached out a hand to pet my hair and face, and after I addressed her as "Auntie," she happily took me in her arms and dandled me on her knee. These friendly gestures settled my father's nerves and gave him a glimpse of what happy married life could be.

They began to date, in encounters not involving me, I being left on such occasions with Hao Qiangsheng and Li Yuezhen. The dates took the form of evening strolls along the railroad line. My father was a bashful, introspective man, and he would escort his partner back and forth without saying a word. Typically it would be she who broke the silence with a remark or two, and only then would he say something, but often his words were drowned out by the roar of an approaching train.

At first their dates were of short duration; they would end after just one or two turns along the tracks, and then my father would come to collect me. Later, the pair would take five or six turns and keep walking until after midnight, by which time I would be sound asleep alongside little Hao Xia, who was three days older than me. Hao Qiangsheng himself, unable to keep his eyes open, would have lain down in bed and begun to snore. Only Li Yuezhen would be sitting patiently in the outside room waiting for my father to arrive. She would briefly inquire about the progress of the relationship before she let my father carry me off. In those days I would often fall asleep in the evening on the bed in Hao Qiangsheng's apartment and wake up in bed in my own house.

This situation continued for two months or so, after which Li Yuezhen felt that my father and the young woman were not making any real progress but simply spending more time on their walks. After she questioned my father closely about the nature of their exchanges, she discovered where the problem lay. By the end of the evening, after all their walking, the girl would be tired. She would come to a stop and say "Good night." My father, not knowing quite what to say, would simply nod, then turn around and head off quickly to Hao Qiangsheng's apartment to collect me.

"Why don't you walk her home?" Li Yuezhen asked my father.

"She already said good night," my father replied.

Li Yuezhen shook her head and sighed. When the girl said good night, she told my father, what she was really hoping was that he would see her home. Seeing his confusion, Li Yuezhen took a firm line. "Tomorrow night," she instructed, "make sure you walk her home."

My father was enormously grateful to Li Yuezhen and her husband, for ever since I was born they had never stopped helping the two of us. He followed her advice, silently walking the young woman back to her home after she said good night. Outside her door, in the moonlight, she said good night a second time, and this time she looked radiant.

Their relationship leapt ahead, and now they did not wait until after dark for a surreptitious date but strolled confidently side by side into the park on Sundays. They were now formally in love, and passionately so. They began to meet in the little house that swayed and shook when trains passed, and they probably hugged and kissed, but I suspect they went no further than that.

From dating to full-blown love affair, I was absent from all the proceedings. This reflected Li Yuezhen's view that for me to join the fun would hinder the normal development of the romance, and my appearance should be delayed until the waters had settled in their course. She believed that so long as this girl truly loved my father, she would naturally accept my existence. During this period I was practically living in Li Yuezhen's apartment. I liked this family: I had a close bond with Hao Xia, and Li Yuezhen was like a mother to me.

When things got to the point where my father and the young woman were ready to discuss marriage, they had to bring me into the conversation. Earlier, when they were courting so avidly, I hardly figured in their thinking at all. Now my father began to talk about me in detail, starting with how he'd heard my wailing and picked me up off the tracks, and sharing the highlights of my development these past four years. He spoke as a happy father, and a proud one, relating a wealth of anecdotes that revealed how clever I was, for he thought me the smartest child in the whole world.

Never before had he talked for so long, or so volubly. After an hour or so, his intended said to him coolly: "You shouldn't have adopted this kid—you should have left him with an orphanage."

My father was speechless. The cheerful glow that lit up his features gave way at once to a stiff, pained expression, and that look of distress, rather than passing quickly, settled on his face for some time. His emotions were in turmoil, for he was now deeply in love with the girl, while loving me, of course, too. These were two different kinds of love, and he needed to choose one and abandon the other.

Actually, the young woman wasn't really rejecting me out of hand—she was simply being pragmatic. She was twenty-eight, which in those days counted as very late to be single, and it meant she didn't have many choices of men. In her eyes my father was strong in all departments—his only drawback was that he had adopted a foundling. She pictured how in the future they would have children of their own, and it seemed to her that fitting me into the family would be an awkward proposition. So that's why she said what she did: if they didn't have me to worry about, things would go more smoothly. She wasn't wrong to think that way: they might well have more than two children, and to have a foundling to care for too would impose a heavy burden on a couple with a limited income. Even so, she still accepted my existence—she just felt that my father should have left me with an orphanage at the outset. She was just saying.

My father tended to have a one-track mind, and if an idea that he was set on found obstacles in its way, he would be unable to think of an alternative. And so the idea got fixed in his head that she would never go along with a package deal. Perhaps he was right, for even if she could have brought herself to accept me, in the long run I would have been a flash point for conflict and strife. My father was like a wet towel dripping with emotions: she and I had seized opposite ends of the towel and were wringing it with all our might, and his heart was in torment.

I had no inkling of his struggle and no awareness that now,

when my father looked at me, it was with pity and not with joy. If anything, during these days he seemed to be all the more devoted to me. Although I was now steady on my feet, my father would carry me in his arms as though I couldn't walk properly, and he would put his face close to mine. Always a bit of a penny-pincher, now every day he would buy me two candies, one of which he would slip into my mouth, the other of which he would pop into one of my pockets.

Much as he found it difficult to part from me emotionally, in his mind he was steadily moving in a different direction. Now twenty-five, one way or another my father needed a woman in his life. He loved me, but he needed a woman's love even more. After much agonizing, he chose her and abandoned me.

Early one morning I woke up to find my father sitting on the bed. He leaned over and said softly, "Yang Fei, let's go on a train ride."

Although I had lived four years next to a busy railroad line, I had never once taken a train. I stuck my nose against the windowpane: as the train began to move and I saw the people on the platform quickly receding, I gave a wail of alarm. Then I saw houses and streets retreating rapidly, and fields and ponds as well, but I noticed the farther away things were, the more slowly they retreated.

"Why is it like that?" I asked my father.

"I don't know," he said morosely.

At noon that day we disembarked in a small town and lunched on noodles in a little place opposite the station, my father ordering a bowl of noodles with shredded pork for me and a bowl of plain noodles for himself. I couldn't finish such a big bowl and my father ate the leftovers. Then he had me sit while he asked directions to the orphanage. The first three people he talked to said they weren't sure; the fourth thought for a moment and then told him where to find it.

He carried me a long way, until we arrived at a stone-slab bridge over a dry riverbed. He heard children singing in a building on the opposite bank and assumed it was the orphanage (it was actually a kindergarten). Clasped in his arms, I heard the singing too. "Dad, there are lots of kids there," I piped up happily.

My father bowed his head and looked around. Next to the bridge was a copse of trees interspersed with rocks and clumps of grass. The biggest rock was dark and flat, and he wiped it with his hand, clearing away little stones as though burnishing a piece of metalwork with sandpaper. Once its surface was clean and shiny, he lifted me up and deposited me on the rock, then brought out a handful of candy from his pocket and put it in mine. I was delighted to see so much candy, and what pleased me even more was that he then filled my other pockets with cookies. Then he unhitched his army canteen and hung it around my neck. He stood in front of me, his eyes fixed on the ground. "I'm leaving now," he said.

"All right," I told him.

My father turned and left, not daring to look back. Only when he was about to disappear around a corner could he no longer restrain himself; he cast a glance back and saw me sitting on the rock and happily swinging my little legs in the air.

It was evening by the time my father arrived back in our town. After getting off the train, he did not go to his own house but presented himself at the young woman's home. He called her out and then headed off toward the park without another word. Accustomed as she was to his taciturn ways, she followed behind. Finding the park closed, he marched around the perimeter wall until they reached a quiet spot, and there he came to a halt and told her everything he'd done that day. The young woman was stunned and even a bit frightened, finding it hard to believe that he would just abandon me like that. Then she realized that he had done this out of love for her, so she hugged him tightly and kissed him with abandon, and he hugged her back, just as tightly. Dry kindling met hot fire, and they agreed to marry the very next day. After further embraces, my father said he was tired and returned to his cabin next to the railroad.

That night he could not sleep. It was the first time the two of us had ever been separated, and he began to be anxious and afraid, not knowing where I was at that moment and not knowing whether the people at the orphanage had discovered me or not. If they hadn't, I might well be still sitting on that rock, and maybe a wild dog would pick up my scent as the night deepened. . . .

The following day, my father, racked with worry, walked with his fiancée toward the marriage registry office. She did not realize that a drastic shift was taking place in his mind; she was thinking only that he looked unusually worn out. When she asked tenderly why this was, and he answered that he had not slept a wink, she attributed this to excitement and a sweet smile came to her lips.

Halfway to the registry office, my father said he needed a rest. He sat down by the sidewalk and put his hands on his knees. Then he buried his head in his arms and burst out sobbing. The young woman had not expected this at all. She stood there dumbly, as a deep unease began to settle over her. Suddenly my father stood up. "I have to go," he said. "I have to go back for Yang Fei."

I didn't know that I had been abandoned—he related all these scenes to me subsequently, and only later did I find traces of this episode deep in my memory. I remember that I was very happy in the beginning, for the whole afternoon I sat on that rock eating cookies and candy. When the children from the kindergarten walked past after school, I was still eating these little snacks. The children were green with envy, and I heard them tell their parents: "I want a candy," "I want a cookie." Later, the sky darkened and I heard a dog barking nearby and I began to feel frightened. I climbed down from the rock and hid behind it, but was still afraid, so I picked up fallen leaves and covered myself with them until even my head was concealed, and only then did I feel safe. I fell asleep under the protection of the leaves, and in the morning it was the voices of the children on their way to the kindergarten that awakened me. Between the gaps in the leaves I saw the sun come up; then I climbed back onto the rock and sat there to wait for my father. I sat for a long time and it seemed that someone came over to talk to me, but I don't remember what the person said. Now I had no candy and no cookies and just a little water in the canteen, so when I got hungry all I could do was drink a couple of mouthfuls of water, and then there was no water either. I was hungry and thirsty and tired, so I climbed down from the rock, lay down in the long grass, heard dogs barking, and covered myself up once more with leaves from head to foot, and then I fell asleep.

My father arrived in the town at midday and ran all the way to where he had left me. From a distance he could see no sign of me. His running steps gradually slowed and he came to a halt not far from the rock, looking around despairingly. Just as he was in an agony of anxiety, he heard me murmur something in my sleep:

"How come Dad's still not here?"

My father told me later that when he saw how I had made

a quilt out of leaves, he first laughed, then wept. He pushed aside the leaves and when he picked me up out of the grass I was already awake and was calling happily, "Dad, there you are! Daddy, there you are at last!"

My father's life and mine once more were intertwined. After this he gave up on marriage—meaning, first of all, that he gave up on the girl with the long braid. She was very upset and couldn't understand it at all; she went running over to Li Yuezhen to pour out her woes. Only then did Li Yuezhen realize what had happened. She gave my father quite a talking-to, pointing out that she and Hao Qiangsheng would have been perfectly willing to adopt me, for she thought of me as her own son, since I had drunk her milk. My father nodded in embarrassment and admitted he had shown poor judgment. But when Li Yuezhen insisted that he make up with the young woman, my father dug in his heels, convinced that he had to choose between the two of us. "All I want is Yang Fei," he insisted.

No matter how Li Yuezhen tried to persuade him, my father responded with total silence. Angry but powerless, all she could do was vow never again to involve herself in his affairs.

Later, I saw that young woman with the long braid several more times. If I spotted her in the street as my father and I were out walking together, I would tug my father's hand and give a cheerful shout of "Auntie!" My father bowed his head and just kept on going, clutching my hand tightly. At first the young woman would still give me a smile, but later she would pretend not to have seen us and not to have heard my call. Three years later, she married a PLA company commander ten years her senior and moved as a military dependent to the faraway north.

After this my father simply devoted himself to raising

me, without entertaining any further romantic aspirations. I was his everything. Relying on each other, we led a life that passed slowly at the time but in retrospect was over very quickly. He recorded my growth, having me stand up against the wall every six months and using a pencil to mark one line after another above my head. When I was in middle school, I quickly grew taller, and when he saw wider and wider gaps between the lines, a blissful smile would appear on his face.

By the time I was in the first year of high school, I was already about the same height as my father and would often beckon him with a smile on my face. He would walk over to me, chuckling, and I would stand up straight and compare our heights. As I steadily grew taller and he steadily got shorter, I continued this practice until the final year of high school, when I could clearly see the strands of white hair on the top of his head and I noticed the wrinkles on his face. With all the work of caring for me, my father looked ten years older than his actual age.

By then my father was no longer a switchman. Manually operated switches had been replaced by electric points and the railroad had become automated. It took a long time for my father to adapt to his new job as a station attendant. He enjoyed responsibility, and when he was a switchman he'd invested all his attention in his work, for if he had made an error in setting the points, a major accident would have ensued. Once he became a station attendant, he had less pressure weighing on him, but the humdrum routine often made him feel that his talents were underused.

The cabin gradually faded into the distance and the two wavering rails did not return. I continued to linger in my own traces, and I felt tired, so I sat down on a rock. My body felt like a quiet tree. My memory trotted slowly through that world I had left, as though on a marathon course.

Through thrift and self-denial my father saw me from primary school through to university. Although in material terms our life was impoverished, it was warm and idyllic in its emotional tenor. One day, however, my birth mother came from afar in search of me, and our calm life was shattered. I was in the final year of university then; my mother came looking for me by retracing her original route and stopping at one town after another. It was her second attempt to find me. On that day forty-one years ago, by the time she had recovered from her fainting spell, the train had already traveled another hundred miles. All she remembered was giving birth to me when the train left a station, but she had absolutely no recollection of which station it was. She had asked people to conduct inquiries at three stations she had passed, but they had not found any sign of me. For a while she thought I must have been run over by the train or had died of hunger on the tracks or had been carried off by a wild dog, and for this she had wept in despair. Later she gave up trying to find me, but in her heart there always remained a sliver of hope—the hope that a kindhearted person would have found me and adopted me, supporting me until I grew up. At age fifty-five, when she retired, she decided to come south herself to look for me, and if she hadn't found me this time she would probably have truly put this thought behind her. Our television and newspapers threw their weight behind her search, for my remarkable birth was truly an appealing catch line, and television and newspapers made hay out of the story of my birth; one headline described me as "the boy a train gave birth to."

In the paper I saw a picture of my weeping mother and on TV saw her tearful recitation, and already I had a presentiment that the child she was searching for was me, because the date that she mentioned was precisely the date that I was born. But on an emotional level I was not particularly perturbed by this development, feeling that this was somebody else's story. What intrigued me, actually, was the difference between her shedding of tears in the newspaper photograph and that on TV: in the photo her tears were stationary, stuck firmly to her cheeks, whereas on TV her tears were in motion, streaming down to the corners of her mouth. For twenty-two years Yang Jinbiao and I had clung to each other through thick and thin, and the only mother I was used to was Li Yuezhen. Now, when another, unfamiliar mother came into the picture, I had a strange feeling of dissonance.

Reading the papers and watching the TV, my father closely followed her accounts of what had happened and became certain that I was the child she was looking for. From information provided by the paper, he knew which hotel she was staying in, so he placed a call from the station office and soon was talking directly to her. After a quick exchange of information they found all the details matched. She started sobbing and he started crying, but they managed to carry on talking on the phone for over an hour, my father fielding a constant stream of questions about me. They arranged to meet at her hotel that afternoon, and when my father came home he told me with excitement, "Your mom's here looking for you."

He went to the bank and withdrew three thousand yuan—

his entire savings—and took me to the town's biggest shopping mall, which had just opened its doors. He felt that when I met my mother I should be dressed smartly, like a TV star, to show that he had not been mistreating me. In recent years he had hardly ever left the area around the railroad station, and entering this grand six-story shopping center for the first time he gazed around in wonder, muttering to himself, "What a splendid place!"

The first floor was devoted to cosmetics. He sniffed appreciatively. "Even the air smells good here," he told me.

He walked over to one of the counters. "Where will we find name-brand suits?" he asked the girl.

"Second floor," she replied.

Taking my arm he boarded the escalator, as proud and confident as a millionaire. We arrived on the second floor to find a well-known foreign-brand outlet straight ahead. He stopped to examine the prices on several rows of neckties in the entrance display and was rather taken aback. "Two hundred eighty for a single tie," he told me.

"Dad," I said, "you've got it wrong. It's two thousand eight hundred."

The look of surprise on his face turned to one of dismay. Suddenly aware of the limits to his budget, he stood there dumbly. Because he had always lived frugally, even on a meager income he had tended to operate under the illusion that he was quite comfortably provided, and it was only now that he became fully aware of his poverty. He didn't dare step foot inside this name-brand store, and with a new sense of inferiority he asked the hovering shop assistant, "Where will we find a cheap suit?"

"Fourth floor."

Head down, he walked toward the escalator, and as we

rode up together I heard him muttering that my life would have been so much better if I hadn't fallen out of the train. He knew from the media reports that my birth mother had retired with the benefits befitting a deputy office head, and my birth father still held the position of section head. My birth father was actually just a low-level functionary in that northern city, but in Yang Jinbiao's eyes he was a powerful, influential figure.

The fourth floor was all domestic brands, and there he bought me a suit, a shirt, a tie, and a pair of shoes, spending only two thousand six hundred yuan—two hundred yuan less than the price of an imported tie. Seeing how smart I looked in my Western-style outfit, he shed his chastened look of a few minutes earlier and recovered much of his misguided complacency. In high spirits once more, as the escalator slowly descended he gazed haughtily at the foreign model in Western clothes displayed in an advertisement on the second floor, claiming that I looked more stylish in my outfit than the foreigner did in his. "It's true what they say," he added. "Clothes make the man."

At two o'clock that afternoon, my father—dressed in a brand-new uniform—and I—in my suit—arrived at the three-star hotel where my birth mother was staying. On inquiry at the front desk, we were told that my mother had gone out that morning and had not yet returned—perhaps she had gone to the TV studio. The girl at the front desk clearly knew her story. She threw me a glance, not realizing I was actually the main character in that story. We sat down in the lobby to wait. The brown sofa had turned grimy from use, and we sat on it stiffly, concerned that our new clothes might get creased.

Before long a middle-aged woman came in. When she looked in our direction, we recognized her instantly and rose to our feet. She noticed us both and looked at me very intensely when the receptionist told her she had visitors. Although we had arranged to meet in the afternoon, my mother had found she couldn't wait that long, and had gone to the station that morning to look for my father, just when we were in the shopping mall. She had succeeded in talking to Hao Qiangsheng, and had even made the trek to my university and quizzed some of my classmates about my situation. Now she came over, trembling from head to toe, and looked at me so fixedly that I felt her eyes were boring into my face. When she opened her mouth, no words came out—tears simply came to her eyes. Finally, with great effort, she spoke. "You're Yang Fei?" she asked.

I nodded.

"And you're Yang Jinbiao?" she asked my father.

My father nodded too.

Her shoulders began to shake. "You're so like your big brother," she told me tearfully. "But you're taller than him."

Then she threw herself on her knees in front of my father, crying, "I owe you so much! I don't know how to thank you." My father took her arm and led her over to the sofa. She couldn't stop sobbing; he had tears streaming down his face. She thanked him over and over again, and after each "I'm so grateful" she would say, "I don't know how to repay you for all you've done for Yang Fei." Knowing he had forsaken married life for my sake, she burst into another round of sobbing. "You have sacrificed so much for my son—way too much," she said.

This way of putting things didn't sound right to my father. "Yang Fei is my son too," he said, looking at me.

"That's true, that's true," my mother said, rubbing her eyes. "He's your son too, he always will be."

Once the two of them were more composed, my mother

seized my hand and launched into a jumbled, flurried sequence of remarks and questions. Whatever response I gave, she would turn to Yang Jinbiao and cry exultantly, "He sounds just like his brother!"

My looks and my voice left my mother in no doubt that I was the child she had given birth to twenty-two years earlier in the toilet of a moving train.

Later, the results of a DNA test confirmed that I was her son. Then other relatives I had never seen before hurried to join us: my birth father and my older brother and older sister, along with my sister-in-law and brother-in-law. The local media had a field day, with "the boy a train gave birth to" achieving the family reunion that all commentators agreed was the ideal outcome. On TV I made a nervous, uneasy appearance, and in the newspaper I saw my awkward smile.

Fortunately, the excitement lasted only two days, for on the third day the TV and newspapers' love of drama was transferred to an intensive police crackdown on vice and pornography. Under cover of night the authorities had launched spot checks of the city's sauna centers and salons, detaining seventy-eight people suspected of engaging in prostitution— and one of the hookers had turned out to be a man! This person, by the name of Li, had performed so effectively as a drag artist that not one of the hundred or more clients he had serviced during the course of a year had detected his imposture. This sensation became the new focus of media energies, and the various news platforms all dropped the story of "the boy a train gave birth to" to concentrate on the antics of the cross-dressing prostitute. They drew particular attention to the subtlety of his techniques for delivering sexual gratification, but drew a discreet veil over the details. So people in our city speculated with relish as to what these techniques were.

Sleet fluttered in front of my eyes but did not land on me. I knew that it was leaving too. I stayed seated on the rock, and my memory continued its loop through that topsy-turvy world.

Two months after those new relatives of mine returned to their northern city, I graduated from university. When we met, my birth parents had expressed the hope that after graduation I would pursue a career in their part of the country. My birth father said he could continue as section chief for another four years, after which he would have to retire. Taking advantage of the authority he still wielded, he had lined up several good job opportunities for me. Yang Jinbiao approved of this suggestion, conscious that he was an insignificant figure with no connections or clout, unable to help me find my dream job. He believed that if I moved to that northern city, on the other hand, there was every chance of an excellent future. My birth father had proposed this option rather cautiously, fearing Yang Jinbiao would not be pleased, and he stressed that for me to stay where I was would also be fine—he would find a way to establish connections here and make sure I got a good job. To his surprise, Yang Jinbiao readily accepted his first proposal and expressed heartfelt thanks for everything he was doing for me. This ended up putting my birth father at a loss to know what to say, and when Yang Jinbiao realized his embarrassment, he corrected himself: "I shouldn't say thank you, for Yang Fei is your son too."

My birth mother was very touched, and later, when we

were alone, the recollection brought tears to her eyes. "He's a good man—such a very good man," she said to me.

My father knew that winters were severe where I was going, so he knitted me a thick sweater and woolen underwear and bought me an overcoat and a large suitcase. He started packing clothes for all four seasons into the suitcase, but soon took the old items out again and went into town to buy me new ones—I didn't realize at the time that he borrowed money from Hao Qiangsheng and Li Yuezhen to buy me them. Then, on a summer morning, I hauled this suitcase filled with winter clothes—that Western suit was in it too—and followed Yang Jinbiao into the train station. After my ticket had been checked, he handed it to me, urging me to keep it in a safe place and reminding me that it would be inspected again on the train. He looked pensive and said not a word as we waited on the platform, but when my train pulled in he raised his hand and patted me on the shoulder. "When you have a chance," he said, "write me a letter or give me a call to let me know you're all right. Don't make me worry."

As my train left the station, he stood there waving. Although the platform was packed with people, I felt as though he was standing there all on his own.

Later, after he slipped away from me, I would bleakly recall the scene on the platform that summer morning. I had burst into his life all of a sudden when he was just twenty-one, and soon I had filled it up entirely, leaving no space for the happiness that should have been his to squeeze its way in. At last I had reached adulthood, thanks to so much painstaking effort on his part, only for me to abandon him on the platform with hardly a second thought.

In that northern city I began a short and uncomfortable

chapter of my life. I saw very little of my birth father, wrapped up as he was in his work and his business engagements. My now-retired mother, however, kept me company morning to night. She took me to every sight worth seeing, combining these excursions with visits to the homes of a dozen former colleagues, to exhibit her long-lost son. They were happy, no doubt, to see us reunited, but I think their primary reaction was simply curiosity. Glowing with elation, my mother would take her hosts through every step in the saga, her eyes brimming with tears when she got to the more stirring moments. On the first few occasions I was very self-conscious, but later I gradually got used to it. I felt like an article lost and then found, and listened unmoved to my mother's account of the pain of her loss and the joy of her discovery.

When I first arrived in my new home, I seemed an honored guest, for my birth parents, my brother and his wife, and my sister and her husband all regularly asked how I was doing, but by the end of the second week I realized I was beginning to outstay my welcome. We were crowded into a three-bedroom apartment, and the family members who were already there occupied the three bedrooms. I slept on a collapsible bed in the cramped living room, and needed to push the dining table right up against the wall before I could open up the bed. Every morning, my mother would rouse me and ask me to fold up the bed and move the table back into the middle of the room, otherwise people would have no place to eat their breakfast. She apologized for the inconvenience, but assured me that my brother's work unit was about to assign apartments and my brother-in-law's unit was about to do the same; after they moved out, I would be able to have a room of my own.

This new family of mine would often get into arguments.

Brother and sister-in-law would argue, sister and brother-in-law would argue, my birth parents would argue, and sometimes everyone would argue in such a confused medley that I couldn't sort out who was arguing with whom. Once, they got into an argument on my account; it happened when I was about to go for a job interview. My brother said I was getting the thin end of the wedge by having to sleep in the living room and proposed that once I had work and a salary I should rent an apartment outside, and my sister said the same thing. My mother got angry. "You both have jobs and salaries," she shouted, wagging her finger at them, "so why don't *you* go rent an apartment outside?"

My father supported my mother, saying my siblings had been working for several years and had some money in the bank, so they should find a place of their own. So then they argued back, detailing how their classmates' parents had so much pull that they had lined up homes for their children ages ago. My father, livid with rage, cursed my brother and sister for having "wolves' hearts" and "dogs' lungs." My mother delivered a similar accusation but in milder language, cursing them for having no conscience, saying they would never have got their current jobs had my father not pulled strings on their behalf. I stood in the corner and watched in desolation as their argument raged. After this my brother fell out with his wife and my sister with her husband. The two women scolded their husbands for not having enough get-up-and-go, saying how so-and-so's husband and so-and-so's husband in their respective work units were so much more resourceful, acquiring in short order house and car and money. The two men didn't take this lying down: their wives were welcome to get a divorce, they said, and then try their luck landing a man with a house and car and money. My sister ran into her room to draft a divorce agreement, and my sister-in-law did the same. My brother-in-law and brother rushed to put their signatures on the documents. After that there were more tantrums, and threats of suicide. First it was my sister-in-law who ran onto the balcony and prepared to throw herself off, and then my sister followed. My brother and brother-in-law softened at this point, grabbing hold of the two women, appealing to their sense of reason and then admitting their own fault. In front of me, one of the men fell to his knees and the other began to slap his own face. At this point my parents retreated to their bedroom, closed the door, and went to bed, for they were only too familiar with this kind of row.

After all the furor had died down, I stood on the balcony in the quiet of the late evening taking in the splendid night views of this northern city, and I began to miss Yang Jinbiao. Never in his life had he cursed me or beaten me; if I'd acted out of line, he would simply and gently reproach me and give a sigh as though he was the one who'd done something wrong.

The next morning the family reverted to calm, as though nothing at all had happened. After the working members had breakfast and left for their offices, only my mother and I were left sitting at the dining table. She felt embarrassed about the row, but even more she felt misused. She kept complaining, complaining about how my brother and sister and their spouses would eat and drink at her expense, never ever paying a penny for their meals; then she grumbled about how my father had too many parties after work, coming home drunk almost every single evening.

She babbled on and on. "What a mess this family is!" she said. "It's so exhausting, managing this kind of household!"

I waited till she had finished. Then I told her gently, "I want to go home."

She looked blank for a moment, before realizing that the

home I was talking about was not hers but my other one. Tears trickled from her eyes, but she made no effort to dissuade me. "Will you come back to see me?" she said, wiping her cheeks.

I nodded.

"Things have been difficult for you here," she said sadly.

I said nothing.

After living in this new home for twenty-seven days, I took the train back to my old home. When I got off the train, I did not leave the station, but hauled my suitcase through the underpass and looked around for my father on one platform after another. I finally saw him at the far end of platform 4, and when I approached, I found he was giving directions to a confused traveler. When the man said "Thank you" and ran to catch his train, I called out to my father, "Dad."

He froze, and it was only when I called a second time that he turned around and looked at me in astonishment, gazing in equal amazement at my suitcase. He saw that I was wearing the clothes I wore on the day of my departure. I had returned in just the same state as I had left.

"Dad, I'm back," I said.

He understood what this meant. He nodded slightly and the rims of his eyes reddened, then he quickly turned around and continued with his work. Looking at the clock on the platform, I could tell that he would get off work in another twenty minutes, so I lugged my bag over to the steps leading down to the underpass and stood there watching as he applied himself to his various tasks. He gave directions to several travelers, indicating where their carriages were located, and he carried bags for an elderly traveler and helped him onto his train. Once the train had pulled out, he looked up at the clock and saw that it was time to knock off, so he came up to me and, picking up my bag, went down the steps. I reached out to grab it back, but he brushed me away with his left hand. It was as though I were still a child and not strong enough to lift such a large suitcase.

I was back in my own home. By this time we had already left the shack next to the railroad line and moved into a dormitory occupied by railroad employees. There were only two rooms, but they were rooms free of argument.

My father was quite composed, despite my sudden return. Since he had not expected me back, there was nothing much to eat at home, and he suggested that I have a shower while he went to a restaurant nearby and picked up some take-out food. He seldom patronized restaurants, and for him to come back with four dishes all at once was quite a novelty. He hardly said anything as we ate, concentrating mainly on putting bits of food into my bowl with his chopsticks. I didn't say much either, telling him simply that I felt this home of ours was the right place for me. I said it wasn't that difficult for university graduates to find work, and a job that I found here wouldn't be significantly inferior to the job my birth father had in mind. My father nodded as he listened, but he spoke up when I said I would start looking for a job the next day. "What's the rush?" he said. "Take it easy for now."

I learned later from Hao Qiangsheng that after I went to bed that night, my father paid a call on them, bursting into tears as he came in the door and announcing to him and Li Yuezhen, "Yang Fei is back! My son is back!"

In his final days my father believed that the best thing he had ever done in life was to adopt a son named Yang Fei. By that time he had retired and I was a section head in the company. I had saved some money and I planned to buy a new two-bedroom apartment. I spent a weekend with my father looking at a dozen housing developments under construction and took a liking to one particular apartment, so we planned to sell my father's railroad dormitory unit. It had been assigned to him as one of the perks of his job, and now he was free to dispose of it as he chose. With the funds gained from its sale, combined with the money I had put aside over the years, we could purchase a new apartment cash down, without needing to pay a mortgage. My professional success offered some consolation to my father for the disappointment of my failed marriage.

During this period I had a lot of work-related engagements in the evenings, and when I returned home late I would find my father waiting for me with a full dinner on the table. If I wasn't home, he would not eat and could not sleep. So I began to turn down as many invitations as possible and instead went home to keep my father company as he ate and watched television. During my vacation that year, I took him to Huangshan for a holiday—the first and last time that he left home for travel. At sixty, my father was still very fit, and while I was soon panting for breath as we climbed the mountain, he moved as nimbly as a swallow and was able to give me a helping hand on the steepest stretches.

Hao Qiangsheng and Li Yuezhen had also retired. Their daughter, Hao Xia, had gone to graduate school in the United States after she finished university in Beijing, then stayed on in America to work, marrying an American and bearing two attractive children. On retirement Hao and Li planned to emigrate to America, and as they waited for their green card applications to be approved they would often come to visit my father—these were his happiest moments. When I opened the door on my return from work and heard peals of laughter from inside, I knew that they were visiting. Li

Yuezhen would give me a cheerful greeting, "Hi, son," when I appeared in front of them.

Li Yuezhen had always called me "Son," and in my mind she was the only mother I had as I grew up. When I was still sucking my thumb in the cotton sling on Yang Jinbiao's back, she had come almost every day to our shack next to the railroad tracks to breast-feed me. "Formula is never as good as mother's milk," she would say to Yang Jinbiao. In my memory she had always been thin, but according to my father she had once been quite plump—it was from feeding me that she grew slender. My father's claim sounded plausible to me, for in those penniless days the poorly nourished Li Yuezhen breast-fed two young children.

I had always been just as familiar with their family as I was with my own. Much of my time as a young child was spent in their home, for I would eat dinner and sleep there when my father worked the night shift. Li Yuezhen treated me and Hao Xia as though we were siblings, and on the rare occasions when we had a meat dish for dinner she would slip the last morsel of pork or chicken in my bowl and not in Hao Xia's. Once Hao Xia burst into tears, saying, "Mom, I'm the one who's your child!"

"It'll be your turn next time," Li Yuezhen said.

Hao Xia and I had been childhood sweethearts and had privately vowed to marry when we were grown up, so we could always be together. "You can be Dad and I'll be Mom," was how Hao Xia put it. At that point we thought of marriage as a combination of a dad and a mom, but once we understood that marriage is defined more precisely as a partnership of husband and wife, neither of us ever again mentioned our secret agreement and we both forgot it with equal speed.

I never again visited my family in the north, but simply

called them on the phone on major holidays. Usually it was my birth mother who picked up, and after quizzing me about my affairs she would always urge me to look after Yang Jinbiao properly, saying with feeling, "He's such a good man."

My father fell ill the year after he retired. He lost his appetite and rapidly lost weight; the whole day through he felt drained of energy. He kept me in the dark, unwilling to let on that he was battling an illness; he thought he would slowly recover. When he got ill in the past he wouldn't go to see the doctor and refused to take medication, instead depending on his strong constitution to see him through, and this time too he was confident he could fight it off. I was busy at work in those days and didn't notice that my father was losing weight, until one day when I found he was just skin and bones and learned that he had been ill for half a year. I insisted that he go to the hospital for tests, and when the results came out, my hands trembled as they held the report, for my father had developed lymphoma.

I watched helplessly as the malignant cells gradually consumed my father's life. Radiation treatment, surgery, chemotherapy—all these tormented my once-strong father so that when he walked it was with a crooked gait and it looked as though a gust of wind would be enough to blow him over. As a retired railroad worker he could claim reimbursement for a portion of his medical expenses, but these expenses were so enormous that we had to bear the bulk of them, and I quietly sold off his railroad dorm unit. So as to look after him, I gave up my job and bought a small shop near the hospital. My father slept in the back room, while in the front room I sold daily necessities to customers going by, so as to bring in a little income.

My father was upset, for I hadn't consulted him before

quitting my job and selling the property. He knew this was a fait accompli and would often sigh and moan, saying to me in distress, "You've got no house and no job—what will you do in the future?"

I tried to reassure him, saying that once he had recovered I would return to my original employer, start saving once more, and buy a new apartment for him to see out his days peacefully. He shook his head. "Where will you find the money to do that?" he said.

"If we can't afford a full-cash purchase," I told him, "we can always buy an apartment by taking out a mortgage."

He shook his head all the more stubbornly. "Don't buy an apartment. Don't go into debt," he cautioned.

I said nothing more, knowing his mind was made up. Before housing prices skyrocketed I had thought of taking out a mortgage, but my father was daunted by the prospect of owing the bank so much money and I had had to abandon the plan.

It was as though we had returned to the life in that rickety shack next to the railroad tracks. In the evening, after I had closed up shop, the two of us crammed onto the single bed to sleep. Every night, I could hear my father's sighs and groans—the sighs on account of my grim future, the groans in reaction to his own pain. When his suffering was not so acute, we would share memories of earlier days, and at such moments his voice would take on a blissful tone. He would mention little episodes from my childhood, recalling how I would insist he lie next to me and watch me as I fell asleep, how sometimes when he adjusted his position and turned his back to me, I would call again and again, "Dad, look at me, look at me. . . ."

I told my father that I remembered hearing him snoring

when I woke up in the middle of the night when I was small. A few times I didn't hear his snore and was so scared that I started crying, worried that perhaps he had died. I would shake him and shake him, and when he sat up, my tears would turn to smiles and I would say to him, "So you're not dead after all!"

One evening my father neither sighed nor groaned. Instead he talked quietly about some key moments in our lives, such as how he had heard me crying on the railroad track and carried me in his arms to Li Yuezhen's house. It was that evening too that I learned how, when I was four years old, he had abandoned me in order to get married. When he got to this point tears trickled from his eyes and he was stricken with self-reproach, saying over and over again, "How could I have been so heartless?"

I pointed out that I had left him too, joining that family up north, so the score was even. In the darkness he patted my hand, saying that for me to go to the home of my birth parents didn't count as abandoning him.

He gave a little laugh. He recalled how clever I'd been to cover myself with leaves to keep myself warm that time he left me by that dark rock. This comment somehow refreshed my memory, and suddenly I remembered the stones, trees, and grasses, and the barking dog that had made me so fearful. I said it wasn't that I was cold, but that I was afraid, for a dog kept barking constantly.

"No wonder," he said, "that you had leaves over your head as well."

I chuckled, and so did he. "I'm not afraid of dying," he said to me evenly. "I'm not afraid of that at all. What I'm afraid of is not being able to see you."

The next day he left without saying goodbye. He said nothing at all, not leaving even a note, dragging away the little life left in him. In the days that followed I kept kicking myself for being so inattentive. Shortly before this, my father had me take out a new railroad uniform from the wardrobe and put it next to his pillow. I hadn't given this a second thought, assuming he just wanted to admire the last new uniform he had been issued prior to his retirement. But I overlooked his longstanding custom—that he liked to put on a new uniform when faced with some important task.

On the day that my father left home, there was a fire in our city—at a department store just half a mile from my little shop. It was afternoon when I heard news of the disaster, and by then I was in a very anxious state, because my father had yet to return home. A horrible thought came to mind— could he have gone to the department store? It seemed just possible. My birthday was coming up, and my father might well have wanted to buy me a present.

I shut up shop for the night and dashed over to the department store. The silver structure was now reduced to a charcoal hulk, as thick smoke billowed upward. The flames had been largely extinguished, but hoses from a dozen fire trucks were still spurting long jets of water on the charred wreckage. Ambulances lined the street, along with several police cars. Fire ladders were propped up against the building and firemen were already inside searching for survivors. Some of the injured had been carried out and ambulances were speeding off, sirens wailing.

Every intersection next to the department store was crammed with people, and everyone was talking about the fire. Standing among them, I heard only snatches of conversation: some said the fire started around ten in the morning, while others said it started at noon. I shuttled back and forth among the onlookers, listening as they discussed the cause of the fire and guessed the number of casualties; it was dark by the time I returned home.

The TV news that evening had a segment on the department store fire. According to an official source, the disaster was triggered by an electrical short circuit at nine-thirty in the morning. The store had only just opened at the time, the news anchor said, and there were few customers inside. The majority were successfully evacuated and only a handful were trapped. The precise casualty figure was still under investigation, the report said.

My father did not return home that evening, and I was on tenterhooks the whole night. In the morning the TV news had the latest on the department store fire: seven dead and twenty-one injured, with two in critical condition. At lunchtime they released the names of the dead; my father was not among them.

But other reports were circulating on the Internet. Some said there were over fifty dead, while others claimed there were twice that. Many people online criticized the authorities for underreporting the figures, and some noted the Work Safety Administration's definition of accidents: a single episode that caused between three and nine fatalities counted as a "fairly serious" accident; over ten deaths constituted a "serious" accident; and a death toll of over thirty was classified as an "extremely serious" accident. The authorities were castigated for trying to downplay the gravity of the disaster by limiting the reported fatalities to seven. Even if the two in critical condition were to die of their injuries, that would only make a total of nine, confining the fire to the category of "fairly serious" accident and thereby averting any unpleasant repercussions on the career prospects of the mayor, the Communist Party secretary, and other bigwigs.

Rumors were spreading like wildfire on the Internet. Some people said the relatives of the unreported dead had been threatened, while others claimed they had been given huge wads of hush money, and still others listed the names of unreported fatalities—again my father's name was absent.

He had now been gone two days, and I began to mount a search. First I made inquiries at the railroad station, thinking the staff there might have seen him, but I drew a blank. He had become so rake-thin, even people who knew him might fail to recognize him. Then I went to see Hao Qiangsheng and Li Yuezhen, who had just got back from Guangzhou, having passed their visa interview at the U.S. consulate there, and were now attending to the sale of their apartment and preparing to make the long flight across the Pacific to join their daughter. They were shocked by my news. Hao Qiangsheng wouldn't stop sighing, and Li Yuezhen burst into tears. "Son," she said, "he doesn't want to be a burden on you."

The most likely explanation, they felt, was that my father was set on returning to his roots—going back to the ancestral village where he was born and where he grew up. I should try looking for him there, they thought.

I passed the shop on to someone else and took a long-distance bus toward my father's old home. I had visited once when I was small, but my father's parents had no warm feelings toward me, thinking I had wrecked his life. My father had five siblings, but their relationship also was strained. My grandfather had worked on the railroad, at a time when state policy allowed an employee's child to get a job on the railroad if the parent took early retirement. Of his six children, my grandfather selected the youngest—my father—to inherit his position and thereby angered the other five. That's maybe why my father never took me back home a second time.

By now, my grandparents had both passed from the scene. My father's five siblings were still living where they always had, but their children had moved away years earlier. Migrant workers in an assortment of different cities, they had put down roots elsewhere.

I got off the bus in a bustling county seat and took a taxi to my father's village. We rode along a road that was broad and level and paved with asphalt concrete, a huge contrast to its condition on my previous visit, when it was a mud track rutted with holes so big that our car was bouncing around all the time. Just as I was marveling over the progress made, the taxi came to a sudden stop. The asphalt road had come to an end and the crude, potholed surface of the past reappeared in front of me. No county official was going to visit a place this far out in the boondocks, the taxi driver said, so the asphalt ended here. Seeing my bewildered city-boy expression, he explained that country roads are built just for the convenience of leaders when they venture out to conduct inspections. The village that I wanted to go to was another three miles farther on, he said. He pointed down the narrow track ahead. "No leader would dream of going to a godforsaken place like that."

My father's village, when I finally got to it, was nothing like the village that I had visited as a child. That village was skirted by trees and stands of bamboo and several ponds. My cousins and I had shot at the birds in the trees with catapults, and we had rolled up our trouser legs and waded into the ponds to catch little shrimp. In those days, field after field shimmered with rapeseed blossom; the voices of men and women, young and old, mingled with the sounds of chickens and ducks, oxen and sheep; and pigs careened along the paths between the fields. The village now was desolate, the fields lying empty, the trees and bamboos cut down. The ponds had disappeared. The young and able-bodied had all abandoned the village for jobs in the city, and the only people I saw were a few old-timers sitting outside their houses and the occasional toddler wandering around. I was doubtful I would recognize my father's siblings, so when I came upon a hunchbacked old man smoking a cigarette by his front door, I asked him where I'd find Yang Jinbiao's brothers and sisters. He muttered "Yang Jinbiao" a few times before he remembered. He called out to another oldster peeling fava beans across the way, "Here's someone looking for you."

The old neighbor got to his feet and studied me as I walked over, rubbing his hands on his pants in preparation for greeting me. I went up to him and introduced myself as Yang Fei. That elicited no reaction, so I told him I was the son of Yang Jinbiao. "Ah!" he went, then opened his toothless mouth to call his siblings: "Yang Jinbiao's son is here!"

Then he turned to me. "You've grown so tall, I'd never have known it was you."

Four other old folk emerged one by one to join their brother. All five siblings wore cheap polyester clothes, and standing in a group they looked very much alike. They differed only in their heights, like the fingers of a single hand.

They were very pleased to see me. I accepted the cup of tea they poured for me but shook my head at the proffered cigarettes. Almost immediately they began to busy themselves washing and chopping vegetables and fetching wine. Seeing that it still wasn't quite three in the afternoon, I said it was a bit early to start preparing dinner, but they disagreed.

With the passage of years, they were no longer jealous of my father, and they all got a bit red around the eyes when they learned he had disappeared after falling critically ill.

Perhaps because their fingers and palms were so rough, they used the backs of their hands to wipe away their tears. I told them I was looking for my father and thought he maybe wanted to die where he'd been born, but they shook their heads and said he'd never come back again.

In the silence, I stood up and left the rock on which I'd been sitting. Sleet continued to billow, but still it did not fall on me—it simply surrounded me. When I walked on, the sleet opened a passage, and when I looked back, it had closed up again.

On the path of memory I was making my way toward Li Yuezhen.

By the time I returned to the city from my father's village, Li Yuezhen was no more. As she was crossing the road in the evening, she was knocked off her feet by a speeding BMW, and as she lay sprawled on the road she was run over first by a truck and then by a delivery van. In the three short days that I was away, I had lost the mother figure so dear to me.

Hao Qiangsheng was overwhelmed by shock and grief, and his daughter was in transit back from the United States. When I arrived at their house, Buddhist priests were conducting a service to ease the passage of the departed soul. Incense swirled around the room and a yellow cloth lay on the table, with fruit and cakes laid out on top, along with a tablet inscribed with Li Yuezhen's name. Several priests stood in front of the table with their eyes half closed, chanting a sutra in a constant hum, like that of mosquitoes. Hao Qiangsheng sat off to one side with a dull look in his eyes, and I sat down next to him.

The priests perhaps knew that Li Yuezhen had been planning to emigrate to the United States, for after reciting the sutra they told Hao that during the service Li Yuezhen's soul had clambered over his knees and over his shoulders, up and into heaven. The fee for the funeral service was three thousand yuan, they said, but with the outlay of another five hundred yuan they could ensure that Li Yuezhen would be reincarnated in a new body in the United States. Hao Qiangsheng nodded woodenly, so the priests closed their eyes once more and resumed their recitation. This time the reading was short, and though I couldn't make out most of the words I did hear references to America—not the regular Chinese term for it, but the English abbreviation, "U.S.A." The priests said that Li Yuezhen had already begun the journey to U.S.A. and would be there shortly, even faster than if she traveled on a Boeing jet.

Hao Qiangsheng didn't seem to register my arrival, and I had been sitting there for quite some time before he realized who I was. Now he burst into tears and grasped my hand. "Yang Fei," he cried, "you've got to go and see your mom!"

Three days before her death—on the morning I went to the village to look for my father, in other words—Li Yuezhen had stumbled upon a scandal. As she crossed a bridge on her way back home from the market, she saw a number of human fetuses floating in the river below. At first she thought they were dead fish, but couldn't understand why they seemed to have arms and legs. Wondering if her eyes were playing tricks on her, she asked a couple of young people nearby to come over. They said it didn't look like fish, but like babies.

When Li Yuezhen hurried down the steps to the riverside, she could see that they were right. Tiny babies were floating downstream amid a tangle of sticks and leaves, and soon several more babies emerged from the shadows underneath the bridge and bobbed on the sunlit surface. As she strained to make them out, Li Yuezhen stumbled over an obstacle underfoot. She looked down to find three fetuses snagged on the bank.

Li Yuezhen felt it her duty to report this find. Instead of going home, she proceeded directly to the offices of the local newspaper, her basket of groceries under her arm. The guard at the entrance, noting her unprepossessing appearance and suspecting she might be coming to lodge a complaint against the authorities, told her that she needed to go to the Letters and Visits Office of the city government. So she waited outside, and managed to intercept two reporters just arriving for work. They rushed to the scene, by which time both bridge and bank were crowded with people and some were using bamboo poles to maneuver the dead babies ashore.

In the course of that morning the two reporters and a dozen or so locals found twenty-seven babies, both infants and fetuses. The eight infants wore, around their feet, tags on which the name of the city hospital was printed; the nineteen fetuses had no such identification. After taking photos with their mobile phones, the reporters paid a visit to the hospital. They were received warmly by the hospital director, who assumed they had come to interview him regarding new hospital procedures designed to alleviate the difficulty and expense of securing medical treatment. One look at the photos of the dead babies, and the director's smile disappeared. He announced that he had to head off to an important meeting immediately, and he called in a deputy to deal with the reporters. After seeing the photos, the deputy director informed the reporters that he had a meeting at the public health department; he turned them over to the hospital's office manager. After glancing testily at the photos, the office manager identified the foot tags. These infants, he said, had died after failing to respond to treatment; their parents had fled because they couldn't afford to pay the medical expenses. Patients' families were always trying to get out of paying their bills, he groused, generating losses of over a million yuan for the hospital every year. The nineteen fetuses, without tags, had been aborted at the end of the second trimester in order to comply with population-control guidelines. Population control is a national policy, after all, he reminded them condescendingly. The twenty-seven babies were medical refuse, he declared, and the hospital had done nothing wrong: trash has to be dumped, after all.

A directive came down from above, and the newspaper pulled the report that the two journalists had filed. But they wouldn't take this lying down: they posted the story and the photos on the Internet. Public opinion was outraged, and on social media criticism hailed down on our city authorities like a spray of bullets. Only now did the hospital admit it had made a mistake, conceding that it had not done a good job of disposing of medical refuse and saying it had already punished those responsible. For the hospital to repeatedly refer to the dead babies as "medical refuse" enraged the netizens, and in the face of even more virulent commentary the media spokesperson for the city government issued a statement that the twenty-seven medical-refuse objects would be disposed of appropriately. They would be treated as human and cremated, and their ashes would then be buried.

I went to the morgue to pay my respects to Li Yuezhen. The

reception room was lined on all sides with wreaths of flowers, a white ribbon inscribed "In deep mourning for Liu Xincheng" pinned to each wreath. I didn't know who Liu Xincheng was, but with so many people dropping off wreaths, this person clearly had to be either of great wealth or of high rank. I did not see Li Yuezhen, and the rows of wreaths somehow made the reception room look bare and empty. I began to wonder if I had come to the wrong place.

At this point I noticed a small chamber off to one side. When I entered its doorway, I found that a large white cloth had been laid on the floor, and the uneven contours of the cloth made me suspect there was a body underneath. I squatted down and pulled the cloth aside: there was Li Yuezhen. She lay in a white dress with a crowd of dead babies around her, as though she were their mother.

Tears streamed down my face. This woman who had mothered me during my formative years lay there peacefully, her face still maintaining its familiar air. I gazed forlornly at her now-frozen expression and inwardly cried "Mom!" as I wiped away my tears.

Late that night, a sinkhole suddenly opened up. Hospital staff on duty at the time, along with some patients and local residents, heard an almighty roar, and people rushed out in panic, thinking there had been an earthquake, to discover that the morgue had been sucked down a huge hole. The sudden appearance of this gaping pit inspired widespread panic. Fearful of being trapped indoors, patients and local residents crowded onto the streets; only those critically ill remained in their sickbeds, leaving their fate to the hand of providence.

The evacuees, though still shaken, began to feel grateful to Old Man Heaven, saying he had a good eye, letting the morgue collapse but sparing the taller buildings nearby—if that sinkhole had moved a few hundred feet to one side or the other, a big building would have collapsed and the death toll would surely be horrendous. "Oh, thank you, Lord!" people mumbled, and one tearful old man added, "What could collapse did, and what couldn't collapse didn't. Old Man Heaven is really on our side."

Panic, after spreading the whole night through, began to recede with the light of day. The city government attributed the sinkhole—measured as a hundred feet wide and fifty feet deep—to excessive pumping of groundwater. Five inspectors were lowered into the hole by ropes, and an hour later they emerged to report that the interior of the morgue was still intact, but the walls and ceiling had developed cracks.

Spectators arrived in throngs. They stood next to where the morgue had once been and admired the hole. "It's practically a perfect circle," they marveled, "as though drawn in advance with a compass! Even old wells are not this round."

It was a couple of days before people remembered that Li Yuezhen and the twenty-seven babies had been laid out in the morgue, but the inspectors said they had not found a single corpse. Li Yuezhen and the dead babies had mysteriously disappeared.

A reporter interviewed the hospital staff member responsible for cleaning the morgue, and he said that when he left work that afternoon they were all still lying in that chamber. Had they been cremated? the reporter asked. The staff member said no, that the funeral parlor did not operate in the evening and no cremations would have been done. The reporter then went to the hospital office, and the people there could not explain how Li Yuezhen and the babies had vanished. It's just too peculiar, they said: surely corpses can't climb out of a hole and slip away by themselves.

Hao Xia, just off the plane and in the throes both of grief

and jet lag, came with her father to the hospital, hoping for a last glimpse of her mother, but the staff had to tell her they did not know where she was.

News of the mysterious disappearance of Li Yuezhen and the twenty-seven babies spread throughout the city and appeared on the front pages of several websites. As interest grew, rumors flew, and on the Internet people freely speculated that there must be some awful secret lying behind all this. Although the local media kept silent, having been ordered to refrain from any reporting, media outlets based elsewhere were eager to make the most of this story, sending their reporters in by plane and train and car, and getting all set to provide saturation coverage.

At a hastily arranged news conference, an official from the civil administration bureau announced that Li and the babies had been sent to the funeral parlor for cremation on the afternoon before the collapse.

"Were the relatives informed?" a reporter asked.

It had been impossible to contact the babies' relatives, the official said.

"What about Li Yuezhen's relatives? Couldn't you contact them?" the reporter asked.

The official was lost for an answer. "Thank you, everyone," he said. The news conference was over.

Late that afternoon the civil administration official and a hospital representative delivered an urn to the Hao family, saying that they had made the decision to cremate because the weather was hot and Li Yuezhen's remains could not be easily preserved. Hao Xia, though she had not slept for over thirty hours, still had her wits about her. "It's only spring now!" she cried furiously.

The morgue attendant then changed his story, claiming that Li Yuezhen and the babies had indeed been sent to the funeral parlor for cremation, and he himself had helped load them into the hearse. Soon, someone who said he worked for a bank put up a post on the Internet, disclosing that five thousand yuan had been deposited in the attendant's personal account that day—hush money, he suspected.

So as to calm such rumors, the city government asked the journalists to come to the funeral parlor to inspect a line of twenty-seven tiny urns, explaining that all the babies had been cremated and would shortly be buried. But with this matter apparently settled, a further wrinkle emerged, for somebody soon reported that the urns of Li Yuezhen and the babies were actually filled with the ashes of other people cremated on that same day. When the relatives of those cremated that day got wind of this, they rushed to open their urns and soon became convinced that a lot of ash was missing, even though they weren't sure just how much ash was normal. One reporter made a point of going to the funeral parlor, hoping that someone there would be brave enough to stand up and admit that the ashes had been tampered with. But all the workers denied this categorically and their leaders dismissed it as Internet rumor. One joke making the rounds in cyberspace was that the funeral parlor workers were definitely going to get a jumbo-sized bonus this month.

I disentangled myself from memories that were now growing tight and thick, as though threading my way out of a forest dense with vegetation. Weary thoughts lay down and rested, but my body continued to move through a boundless void, an empty silence. In the air no birds circled and in the water no fish swam and on the earth nothing grew.

THE FOURTH DAY

I continued to roam between morning and night, with neither burial plot nor cinerary urn, and no clear direction to a place of rest. There was neither snow nor rain, and all I saw was air in motion, like gusts of wind that blow this way and that.

A young woman—another wanderer, by the look of it—walked past me, in the direction from which I had come. I turned and looked at her; she turned and looked at me. Then she walked back and scrutinized my face. Her voice was as fleeting and insubstantial as mist. "Where have I seen you before?" she said inquiringly

That was my question too. I studied this vaguely familiar face. Her hair was fluttering, but I didn't feel the swishing of the breeze—for I had noticed bloodstains around her ears.

"I've seen you somewhere," she said.

Her question had become a statement, and in my memory her face began to look more recognizable. I tried to think back, but recovering things from my past had become more and more strenuous, like climbing a mountain.

"The bedsit," she reminded me.

With relief I arrived at memory's peak, and a broader landscape came into view.

⋅〜

Over a year ago, soon after I moved into the bedsit, there lived next door a pair of young lovers, their hair dyed in garish colors. They left early and returned late each day and I didn't know their names and didn't know what kinds of jobs they did. Their hair changed color practically every week: green, yellow, red, brown, multicolored—black was the only color I never saw. However their hair changed color, the two of them always had hair of the same hue—"sweetheart color" was what they called it. After a month I learned that they worked in a hairdressing salon. According to my landlord, they were not actual hairdressers, but simply hairwashers. During my third month at the bedsit, they moved out.

I could hear everything they said and did in the next room, for the wall blocked my vision but presented little obstacle to my hearing. When they made love, their bed rattled and shook and I heard panting and groaning and yelling; almost every evening the room next door would resound with tumultuous noise.

Their shaky finances often led to arguments. Once I heard the girl shouting through her sobs that she wasn't going to go on living with a down-and-outer like him. She wanted to marry the scion of some wealthy family, for that way she wouldn't need to work her fingers to the bone and could just play mahjong every day to her heart's content. The guy said he'd had enough of living in penury with her—he wanted to be partner to some rich lady, live in a villa, and drive a sports car. Each went on and on describing his or her own brilliant prospects as a way of putting the other down, vowing to part company the next day, the sooner to embark on a glorious future. But the next morning they carried on as though nothing at all had happened, leaving their bedsit hand in hand, off to the salon for another long day at their tiring, low-paying jobs.

In their most heated argument, the guy struck the girl. She had been talking about a girlfriend of hers who had left the countryside the same time she did. They were from the same village, it seemed, and this other girl worked behind the counter at a nightclub. When a customer took a fancy to her, she would charge a thousand yuan for sex or two thousand if she spent the whole night with him. She and the nightclub divided the proceeds sixty-forty, sixty percent to her and forty percent to the club, and thus she could earn thirty or forty thousand yuan a month. After three years in the game, she had accumulated a number of regulars who would call her up to arrange a session, and that way she didn't need to share her earnings with the club and could make up to seventy thousand a month. The girl said that her friend had recommended her to the nightclub and the manager was ready to interview her.

"Is that okay with you?" she asked.

He made no reply. She said this was something she wanted to do. She could make a lot of money this way, and he wouldn't have to work—she could support him. After a few years, she said, she'd have put away enough funds that she could quit the racket. They'd go back to his home district, buy a house, and open a shop.

"That okay?" she asked again.

Now he said something. "You'll end up with syphilis, or AIDS."

"No, I won't," she said. "I'll make my clients wear a condom."

"Scumbags like them—they're likely to refuse."

"If they refuse, then I won't let them do it. You're the only man in the world who I'll let do it without a condom."

"No way are you going to go through with this! Even

if I have to starve, I'm not going to let you be a nightclub hostess."

"Well, you can starve to death if you like, but I'm not going to."

"If I say no, it's no."

"Who do you think you are? We're not married, you know—and even if we were, I could always get a divorce."

"I don't want to hear another word about this."

"You'd better get used to the idea. My girlfriend has a boyfriend, and he's willing to go along with it, so why aren't you?"

"Her boyfriend is a piece of shit."

"No, he's not! One time she got bitten by a client, and her boyfriend tracked him down and cursed him as a pervert and beat the hell out of him."

"You have to be a real shit to let your girlfriend be a whore. He can curse the other guy as much as he likes, but he's nothing more than a pimp himself."

"I don't want to keep on living like this, I've had enough! When the iPhone 3 came out, my girlfriend got one right away, and as soon as the iPhone 3s came out, she immediately switched to that. Last year she exchanged it for an iPhone 4, and now she's using an iPhone 4s. Look at this crappy cell phone of mine—I couldn't even get two hundred yuan for it!"

"I'll get you an iPhone 4s, don't you worry."

"You can't even scrounge together the money for three meals a day! By the time you can afford to buy me an iPhone 4s, they'll be selling the iPhone 40s."

"I told you I will get you an iPhone 4s."

"You're not serious, are you? You're just bullshitting me."

"I *am* being serious."

"I can't be bothered to discuss this with you. Tomorrow I go to the club."

The next thing I heard was a series of loud slaps—*bap, bap, bap.*

"Beat me, would you?" she sobbed. "Just beat me to death, why don't you?"

He started crying too. "I'm sorry, I'm sorry!"

"How can you dare beat me?" she cried. "You're always broke, but still I stay with you, because I thought you would treat me right. And now you beat me! You're a brute!"

"I'm sorry, I shouldn't have done that!" he wailed.

Again I heard a series of rapid slaps—it sounded like he was slapping his own face. Then there was the sound of a head hitting a wall—*bang, bang, bang.*

"Don't! Don't do that!" she begged, sobbing all the while. "Stop, please. I won't go to the nightclub. Even if I have to starve, I won't go."

At this point, my memory paused. Looking at this young woman with her desolate expression, I nodded. "Yes, I've seen you before, in the bedsit."

She smiled faintly, but her eyes were anxious. "How long have you been here?" she asked.

"Three days." I shook my head. "Maybe four."

Her face fell. "I've been here three weeks."

"You have no burial plot?" I asked.

"No, I don't. How about you?"

"I don't, either."

She raised her head and scanned my face carefully. "Have you done something with your eyes and nose?"

"Yes, and my chin too," I said.

"The chin isn't obvious," she said.

She noticed my armband. "You're wearing that for yourself."

This took me aback. How could she know that? I wondered.

"There are people over there who've done that too," she said.

"Where?" I asked.

"Let me take you," she said. "None of them have burial plots."

I followed as she led me toward a place I'd never been. I knew her name now—not because she told me, but because my memory had caught up with the world that had gone away.

A young woman named Liu Mei committed suicide by jumping off a building, distressed that her boyfriend had given her a knockoff iPhone 4s for her birthday instead of the real thing. This story got blanket coverage three weeks ago.

For three days in a row, the local newspapers carried reports on Liu Mei's suicide—in-depth reports, or so the papers said. The reporters ferreted out many details of Liu Mei's life story, how she met her boyfriend when she was working at the salon, how they had two steady jobs in two years—as hairwashers in the salon and as servers in a restaurant, as well as several temporary jobs; how they rented five different places, at lower and lower rent, the last rental in a basement, a former bomb shelter built during the Cultural Revolution and later converted into as the biggest underground accommodation complex in this city of ours.

The papers said that at least twenty thousand people were living in our city's air-raid shelters, and they were known as "the mouse tribe," for like mice they emerged from holes and crannies and after roaming outside during the day would return at night to their underground nests. The papers published photos of the room where Liu Mei and her boyfriend had lived, separated from their neighbors only by a piece of cloth. The papers said that with the mice tribe cooking and going to the bathroom in the air-raid shelters, things got terribly filthy. To the reporters, the air was so heavy it didn't feel like air at all.

One discovered the log of Liu Mei's space on QQ, the instant messaging service, and learned that her username was Mouse Girl. In the period leading up to her suicide, she had announced her receipt of a birthday present from her boyfriend. He said he'd spent over five thousand yuan to get it. The two of them had celebrated with dinner at a food stall, but the following day her boyfriend had to rush home to see his father, who was seriously ill. She got together with a girlfriend, the owner of a genuine iPhone 4s, and compared their two phones, discovering that the bitten-into apple on her own phone was a bit bigger than that on her friend's, and that her phone was noticeably lighter in weight, although the clarity of the touch screen was similar. Only then did she realize that her boyfriend had tricked her—this phone was a knockoff, and couldn't have cost more than a thousand yuan, tops. Someone who knew a lot about these things left a post on her log, noting that if the resolution of the touch screen was high, then it sounded like a Sharp product. He used the term "resolution" rather than "clarity" and corrected her use of the term "knock-off phone," saying that if it had a Sharp touch screen it should be termed "a superior imitation" and it would have cost more than a thousand yuan.

Mouse Girl's boyfriend's cell phone had its service suspended because money was owed on the account, so she couldn't reach him directly, and all she could do was sit in an Internet cafe, calling him on her QQ space for five days in a row and demanding that he get his ass back right away. By the fifth day her boyfriend still had not responded, so she cursed him as a spineless coward, then announced that she wanted to die, and made public the time and place of her intended suicide: noon the next day, on one of the bridges over the river. But someone on the Internet urged her to think of some other way, since it was midwinter and the river was so cold it would be excruciatingly painful; she should find a warm place to commit suicide, for you need to be good to yourself even when taking your own life. She asked for suggestions, and this person recommended that she buy a couple of bottles of sleeping pills, swallow them all at one go, wrap herself in her comforter, and dream away happily until she died. Other commenters thought this a lousy idea, because her doctor would give her at most a dozen or so pills for each prescription, and if she wanted to get two full bottles' worth she would need to postpone her suicide by a good six months. She was not going to delay her suicide, she declared; instead she had decided to throw herself off a building—the apartment building opposite her underground home. When she named the location, two residents asked her not to die just outside their front door, for this would bring them bad luck. One of them suggested she find a way to climb up onto the roof of the city government headquarters and jump off from there, arguing that this would really make a statement, but others ruled that out, since there were military policemen guarding the entrance to the city government headquarters and they would detain her as a suspected petitioner before she even got through the front door.

She decided in the end to make her leap from the Pengfei Tower—at fifty-eight stories the tallest building in town. This time no netizen opposed her plan—indeed, some praised this as an excellent choice, saying that before dying she could enjoy the stunning view. The last line that she left in cyberspace was addressed to her boyfriend. "I hate you," she said.

Mouse Girl killed herself in the afternoon. I happened to be at the Pengfei Tower just at that time, carrying my university diploma in my pocket, because I had learned that several companies handling English tutorial services were based in the Pengfei Tower, and I wanted to see if I could find a position as a tutor.

There was a huge crowd out in front. Police cars and ambulances were there too, and people had their mouths hanging open as they gazed up at the skyscraper. This was right after the first heavy snow of winter; the snow gleamed in the bright sunshine, under a blue sky. A tiny figure could be seen some thirty stories up, perched on a wall. Before long the glare of sunlight became uncomfortable, and I had to lower my gaze and rub my eyes. Others did the same, craning their necks and then lowering their heads and rubbing their eyes, before looking up once more. Amid a clamor of commentary, I heard that the girl had been standing there for over two hours.

"Why is she standing there?" someone asked.

"She's going to jump off," another said.

"Why does she want to do that?"

"She's tired of living, I guess."

"Why?"

"Hell, that's not so hard to figure out, is it? So many people these days are tired of living."

Petty tradesmen and street vendors arrived on the scene, squeezing in and out among the throng, flogging wallets and bags, necklaces, scarves and whatnot, all knockoff versions of name brands. Some were selling "happy oil."

"What's happy oil?" somebody asked.

"A quick rub and you'll have a hard-on" was the reply. "Firm as iron, hard as steel, more virile than Viagra."

Some were offering spying paraphernalia. "Do you want a bugging device?" they asked in a low voice.

"What would I do with one of those?" someone asked.

"You can check whether your wife has taken a lover."

Another vendor was selling sunglasses. "Ten yuan a pair!" he shouted, and recited a little jingle for good measure: "You can see far, you can see high, no need to fear the sun in your eye."

Some people bought sunglasses and put them on right away, so they could focus more intently on the tiny figure high up on the Pengfei Tower. I heard them say that they could see a policeman sticking his head out of a window next to the girl. He must be trying to talk her out of it, they said. A minute later, the spectators wearing the ten-yuan sunglasses began to shout: "The policeman is sticking his arm out!" "And the girl is sticking hers out, too!" "She must have changed her mind." But almost immediately there was a uniform chorus of "Ah!" and then a sudden hush, and moments later I heard a heavy thump as the girl's body hit the ground.

The last sight that Liu Mei left in that world was a spurt of blood from her mouth and ears. And the force of the impact split the legs of her jeans wide open.

"You can still call me Mouse Girl," she said. "Were you there when I fell?"

I nodded.

"Someone said I was a terrible sight, with blood all over my face. Is that true?"

"Who said that?"

"Someone who came over later."

I said nothing.

"Was I really that scary?"

I shook my head. "When I saw you, it was as though you were sleeping, meek and mild."

"Did you see any blood?"

I hesitated, reluctant to mention it. "Your jeans split open," I said.

She gasped with surprise. "He didn't tell me that."

"Who didn't?"

"The man who came later, I mean."

I nodded.

"My jeans split open," she murmured. "In what way?"

"They split into strips."

"What do you mean?"

I thought for a moment. "A bit like the strips of a cotton mop."

She looked down at her pants, a pair of long, wide pants—men's pants.

"Somebody has changed my pants," she said.

"They don't look like yours."

"You're right," she said, "I don't have any pants like this."

"Some kind person must have done that for you," I said.

She nodded. "How did you come over?" she asked.

I thought back to that last scene in the Tan Family Eatery. "I was eating noodles in a restaurant and reading a newspaper when the kitchen caught on fire. There was an explosion, and I don't remember anything after that."

"You'll hear the rest of it from one of the later arrivals," she said knowingly. "I didn't really want to die," she added. "I was just angry."

"I know," I replied. "When the policeman stretched out his hand, you stretched out yours."

"You saw that?"

I didn't, but the people with the ten-yuan sunglasses did. I nodded all the same, to confirm that I saw it.

"I'd been standing there a long time, and the wind was so strong and so cold, I maybe just got frozen stiff. I wanted to grab his hand, but my foot slipped—I might have stepped on some ice. . . . There was saturation coverage in the papers, I'm told."

"For three days," I said. "No more than that."

"That's still a lot. What did the papers say?"

"They said your boyfriend gave you a knockoff iPhone, not a real one, and so you killed yourself."

"That's not right," she said. "The thing was that he deceived me, claiming it was a real iPhone when it was a fake. If he hadn't given me anything, I wouldn't have got mad. I just couldn't stand him lying to me. The papers are just making things up. What else did they say?"

"They said that after giving you the fake iPhone your boyfriend went back home to tend to his father."

"Well, that was true." She nodded. "But I didn't kill myself over some fake merchandise."

"The journal you had on your QQ space was published in the papers too."

She sighed. "I wrote that for him to read, and wrote it that way on purpose, because I wanted him to come back right away. I would have forgiven him if he had just apologized."

"But instead you climbed to the top of the Pengfei Tower."

"He never had the guts to respond to me. The only thing

I could think of was to climb the Pengfei Tower. That would make him show up, I thought."

She paused for a moment. "Did the papers say anything about him being upset when I died?"

I shook my head. "They had no news about him."

"The policeman told me my boyfriend had rushed back and was down below, in an awful state." She looked at me, perplexed. "That's why I reached for the policeman's hand."

I hesitated for a moment. "He didn't come, I don't think. At least, none of the papers said he had."

"So the policeman lied to me too."

"He said that to save you."

"I know." She gave a little nod. "Did the papers mention him later?"

"No."

"He kept his head down the whole time, the little creep," she said bitterly.

"Maybe he never heard," I said. "Perhaps he never went online and never saw what you wrote in your journal. He wouldn't have seen our papers where he went."

"That's true," she admitted. "He can't have known."

"He must know now," I said.

I walked with her a long way. "I'm tired," she said. "I'd like to sit down on a chair."

The open land on all sides created an enormous emptiness around us, and the sky and the earth were all we could see. There were no trees in the distance and no river flowing; we heard no rustle of breeze through the grass and no sound of footsteps.

"There are no chairs here," I said.

"I'd like to sit down on a wooden chair," she continued. "Not a concrete one or a metal one."

"You can sit down on whatever kind of chair you like," I said.

"I already have the chair in mind," she said, "and I'm already sitting on it. It's a wooden bench. You have a seat, too."

"All right," I said.

As we walked, we sat on the wooden bench that we had imagined. She seemed to be sitting at one end and I at the other, and I felt her looking at me.

"I'm tired," she said. "I feel like leaning on your shoulder. . . . Forget it, you're not him. I can't lean on your shoulder."

"You can lean on the back of the bench," I said.

As she walked, she leaned back. "I'm leaning against the back of the bench," she said.

"Do you feel better now?"

"Yes, I do."

We walked on in silence, and it seemed as though we were relaxing on a wooden bench.

A good deal of time seemed to pass, and in her imagination she rose from the bench and said, "Let's go."

I nodded, and together we left the bench of our imagination.

It seemed as though we were walking on at a more rapid pace.

"I've been looking for him all this time," she said morosely. "But I can't find him anywhere. By now he should know what happened to me. He won't be lying low any more, surely. He must be looking for me."

"The two of you are separated now," I said.

"What do you mean?"

"He's there and you're here."

She bowed her head. "That's true," she said.

"He must feel terrible," I said.

"He's bound to," she said. "He loved me so much, he must be looking for a burial plot for me now, so I can have a good resting place."

Saying this, she gave a sigh. "He's got no money," she went on. "And his friends are just as poor as he is. How will he work up the money to buy me a burial plot?"

"He'll think of something."

"That's true," she said. "He'd do anything for me, and he'll figure it out."

A smile of relief appeared on her face, as though she had recovered a sweet memory from that departed world.

"He used to say I was the prettiest girl in town," she murmured. "Is it true that I'm pretty?"

"You're very pretty." I was sincere.

She smiled happily, but then a vexed look crept over her face. "I'm worried," she said. "Spring is coming, and then summer. My body will rot and then I'll just be a bunch of bones."

"He'll get you a burial plot soon," I reassured her. "That way you'll have a resting place before spring arrives."

"You're right." She nodded. "That's what he'll do."

We walked on in silence, the silence of death. We said nothing more, because our memories made no further progress. Those memories of a departed world were of many colors, empty but also real. I felt the silent motion of the desolate young woman by my side and sighed over the heartache that other world had left her with.

Then it seemed we had reached the end of the open country. She came to a halt. "We're here," she said.

To my amazement I now saw another world, one where streams were flowing, where grass covered the ground, where trees were thick with leaves and loaded with fruit. The leaves were shaped like hearts, and when they shivered it was with the rhythm of hearts beating. I saw many people, some just bones, some still fleshed, walking back and forth.

"Where are we?" I asked.

"This is the land of the unburied."

Two skeletons sitting on the ground playing chess blocked our path, as though a door were in our way. We stood in front of them as they argued, each accusing the other of trying to take back his move. The sounds of their quarrel continued to escalate, like flames that rise higher the more they leap.

"I'm not playing with you anymore!" the skeleton on the left said, making a gesture of tossing aside the pieces.

The skeleton to the right made an identical gesture. "Well, I'm not playing with you!"

Mouse Girl spoke up. "Stop quarreling, you two! You were both trying to change your moves."

They stopped arguing and looked up at her, opening their empty mouths. That must mean they're smiling, I thought. Then they noticed there was someone else next to Mouse Girl, and two pairs of empty eyes began to take stock of me.

"Is this your boyfriend?" the one on the left asked.

"Your boyfriend's too old for you," the one on the right said.

"He's not my boyfriend," said Mouse Girl. "He's not old, either. He just got here."

"I could tell that from the flesh on him," the one on the right said.

"You must be in your fifties, right?" the one on the left said.

"Forty-one," I answered.

"Impossible!" said the one on the right. "You must be at least fifty."

"No, I really am forty-one," I said.

"He knows our story, right?" Left Bones said to Right Bones.

"He ought to, if he's that age," Right Bones said.

"Do you know our story?" Left Bones asked.

"What story?"

"Our story over there."

"There are lots of stories over there."

"Yes, but ours is the most famous."

"What story's that?"

I waited for them to tell me their story, but they stopped talking and concentrated on their chess game instead. Mouse Girl and I took a step over the gap between them, as though we were stepping over a threshold.

Mouse Girl and I walked forward together. I looked around me as I went, and it felt as though the leaves were beckoning, the stones were smiling, the river was saying hello.

Skeletal people approached us from the river, from the grassy slopes, and from the woods. They nodded to us gently, and though they brushed past without stopping, I could see their attitude was friendly. Some greeted us warmly, one asking if Mouse Girl had found her boyfriend, another asking if I had just arrived. It was as though their voices had meandered about before coming to my ears, bringing with them the moisture of the river, the freshness of the grass, and the swaying of the leaves.

Now once more we heard an argument erupt between the chess players. It exploded in the air like a firecracker, but it sounded empty, like a quarrel and nothing more.

Mouse Girl told me they were both unreasonable when playing chess, constantly retracting their moves as they played, then getting into a row. Over and over again they would vow to abandon the game, go off to get cremated, go off to their respective graves, but neither of them had ever once stood up when saying this.

"They have burial places?"

"Yes, they both do," Mouse Girl said.

"Why don't they go?"

All Mouse Girl knew was that they had been here for at least ten years. The one surnamed Zhang had been a policeman. He wouldn't get cremated, and wouldn't go to his burial place, because he was waiting for his parents over there to secure the title of "martyr" for him. The other one, surnamed Li, wouldn't get cremated or be buried either, because he wanted to keep Zhang company. Li said that once Zhang got approved to be a martyr, then the two of them together—close as brothers, since they were—would proceed to the crematorium oven and each would move on to his own resting place.

"I heard that one of them killed the other," Mouse Girl said.

"I know their story," I said.

More than ten years earlier, after my birth parents arrived from that northern city to claim me and the tale of "the boy a train gave birth to" had come to a satisfying conclusion, another story had begun. During "Operation Thunderclap,"

a police-led crackdown on vice in my city, one of the prostitutes caught in the net proved to be a man. Surnamed Li, he had dressed up as a woman to troll for customers.

A young policeman named Zhang Gang, just graduated from police academy, took part in "Operation Thunderclap"; he conducted the questioning the night when Li was brought in. Li showed not the slightest remorse over either his cross-dressing or his flesh-peddling and even showed a fulsome pride in his ingenious technique. According to him, he was a past master at handling those clients of his, and if the police hadn't caught him not a single john would ever have discovered that he was a man. Unfortunately, he had focused too much of his energy on attending to his clients and not taken enough steps to guard against the police. That was how he ended up tumbling into the sewer, he said.

In this, his first-ever interrogation, Zhang Gang was in no mood to be lenient. This fake prostitute was not only failing to be humble and meek, but even had the gall to display the supercilious pride Zhang Gang had thought only instructors at the police academy possessed. Zhang Gang was already seething with righteous indignation, and now, when police custody was compared to a sewer, his patience was pushed beyond its limits. He raised his boot and planted a vicious kick in Li's groin. Li clutched his groin and screamed in pain, rolling around on the floor for minutes on end. "My balls!" he cried. "You've crushed my balls!"

Zhang Gang was unimpressed. "What do you need your balls for, in the first place?"

Li was held in custody for fifteen days, and after his release he began what was to become three years of protests. At the start he would appear at the main entrance to the public security bureau every day without fail, rain or shine, gripping a handwritten sign that read "Give me back that pair of balls!" To make clear that these appendages were not just ornamental but had practical application, he would emphasize to passersby that he used his earnings to sleep with call girls.

Someone pointed out that it was rather crude to write the word "balls" on the sign. He cheerfully accepted this correction, changing it to read "Give me back that pair of testicles!"

"See, I'm using cultured language," he explained to passersby.

Li's prolonged protest created an enormous headache for the public security bureau director and his deputies. It was a real nuisance to see Li holding his sign up outside the front gate every day, especially when their superiors dropped in for an inspection and inquired, "What's all this about testicles?"

After holding a meeting to discuss what to do, the director and his deputies transferred Zhang Gang out of the bureau and into a local police station. Li and his testicular complaint followed him there. A year later, it was the police station commander and deputy commanders' turn to squeal, and they got into the habit of running over to the public security bureau at least a couple of times a week to pour out their woes and present gifts to the bureau chief and his deputies, claiming that it was impossible for their station to operate normally. The chief and his deputies showed due solicitude for their subordinates' predicament, transferring Zhang Gang to the detention center, where he was soon followed by Li and his "pair of testicles." After two years of tearing their hair out, the detention center's chief and deputies brought their story before the bureau chief and his deputies, reporting that every day that pair of testicles was hanging around outside their office, destroying all semblance of legal dignity.

They had put up with this for a full two years, they said, and it was high time the "pair of testicles" were moved somewhere else. The bureau chief and his deputies agreed that the detention center had really had a hard time of it and that Li and his "pair of testicles" indeed ought to find an alternative home. But there wasn't a single police station that was willing to accept Zhang Gang, for everyone was aware that the minute he arrived, so would his unsightly shadow.

Zhang Gang knew that the detention center wanted to get rid of him and that no police station would take him. For his part he was not keen on staying in the detention center, so he went to see the public security bureau chief and applied to transfer back to the bureau. After hearing him out, the bureau chief found that one scene kept coming back to haunt him—that of a "pair of testicles" hanging around there at all hours. He thought things over briefly and asked Zhang Gang if he'd considered changing his profession. Zhang Gang asked what he had in mind. The chief proposed that he resign and open a little shop or something. Once he was no longer a policeman, the chief suggested, that "pair of testicles" might well get off his back. Zhang Gang smiled thinly and told the chief he had only two choices ahead of him: one was to kill Li and be done with it; the other was to stand outside the front door, next to the other protestor, and hold up a sign demanding he be allowed to return to the public security bureau. Tears welled up in his eyes as he spoke. The chief sympathized with Zhang Gang's situation and in any case was about to retire, and once retired he wouldn't care in the least if that "pair of testicles" loitered outside the entrance. He rose to his feet, walked up to Zhang Gang, and patted him on the shoulder. "Come on back," he said.

So Zhang Gang returned to the bureau, but Li, strangely,

failed to follow him. Even after Zhang Gang had been working in the bureau for a month, people in other departments still assumed he was just visiting. Why was he always coming by the bureau, they wondered—what had happened over at the detention center? He had been transferred back, Zhang Gang told them. They were amazed, asking why they hadn't seen that "pair of testicles" at the entrance. The bureau chief and his deputies found this startling too, for that matter, and once during a meeting a deputy chief blurted out, "How come those testicles are not there at the entrance any more?"

Even in their absence, Zhang Gang remained on tenterhooks, and at the beginning and end of every workday his eyes were inevitably drawn to the entrance. Only when he was certain that Li had not appeared was his mind put at rest. At first he was concerned that Li might simply be ill, and that as soon as he recovered he would again come and loiter outside the building. But three months passed, then six, and there was still no sign of that "pair of testicles." Zhang Gang breathed a sigh of relief, feeling at last he could focus on work and resume normal life once more.

It was over a year before Li reappeared, by which time everyone in the bureau had completely forgotten about him. This time he no longer held up a sign that read "Give me back that pair of testicles!" but strode in with a black bag on his back. The guard at the entrance noticed a figure brush past as a van was leaving the compound, and he barked out a challenge. The visitor answered without turning his head, "I've got business."

"Come and sign in," the guard called.

But by then Li was already inside the main building. In the hallway he asked a policeman where he'd find Zhang Gang.

After answering his inquiry, the policeman began to sense there was something familiar about this visitor, but didn't make the connection to the notorious "pair of testicles" of four years earlier. Li didn't take the elevator, fearing he might be recognized, and took the stairs up to the fifth floor. When he entered room 503, there were four policemen sitting there. Li recognized Zhang Gang immediately and opened his black bag as he approached. "Zhang Gang," he said.

Zhang Gang raised his head from the file he was writing in and recognized Li. As he looked at him in confusion, Li pulled out a long knife from his bag and slashed Zhang Gang's neck. A jet of blood spurted out, and Zhang Gang put a hand to the wound, leaning back weakly into his seat. He hardly had time to groan before Li plunged the knife into his chest. Only now did the other three policemen react, charging at Li, who pulled the knife out of Zhang Gang's chest and flailed out at his attackers. They could only use their arms to defend themselves and were soon gashed and bleeding heavily. Fleeing to the corridor, they cried, "Help! There's a killer!"

The fifth floor of the public security bureau was thrown into chaos. Swathed in blood and panting heavily, Li slashed away at anyone within reach. Policemen rushed to the scene from other floors, and it was only when twenty of them set on Li with electric cattle prods that they managed to subdue him. By that time he was leaning against a wall and too weak to put up further resistance.

Zhang Gang died in the ambulance on the way to the hospital. Li was executed six months later.

This case immediately made headline news. Everyone was talking about it, saying how the police like to throw their weight around, but when it comes down to it they are all useless, even a man who's got no balls can slash one of them to death so easily and wound another nine, two seriously. If it had been a crowd of men with balls, they could surely have massacred the entire public security bureau. Hearing these comments, the policemen refused to concede they were at fault, arguing that had they known Li planned to kill people they would have overwhelmed him from the start. People who arrive at the public security bureau with backpacks are normally there to deliver bribes, one policeman pointed out—who could have known that this guy would pull out a knife, rather than a gift?

For over ten years Zhang Gang's parents made efforts to see that their son was awarded the title of "martyr." The city public security bureau objected to this, on the grounds that Zhang Gang did not die in the line of duty. His parents then embarked on a long petitioning effort, appealing first to the provincial public security bureau, then taking things up to the public security ministry in Beijing. The city public security bureau was driven to distraction by the parents' campaign. One year, as China's two major political congresses were being held in Beijing, Zhang Gang's parents unfurled a banner in Tiananmen Square, demanding that their son be recognized posthumously as a martyr. The authorities in Beijing were infuriated, and they subjected their colleagues in the provincial and city public security bureaus to scathing criticism. The city public security bureau changed its tack, submitting a request that Zhang Gang be awarded martyr status. The provincial authorities passed this request on to Beijing, but were stonewalled. Zhang Gang's parents persisted in their appeals, making a particular point of boarding a train to Beijing when the two big meetings of the Communist Party Congress were in session, but they would always be intercepted en route, then held in custody in one small hotel or another and not released until the meetings were over. Once the story of Zhang Gang's parents' petitioning campaign was publicized on the Internet, the city stopped sending agents to intercept and detain them, and changed its tactics. During every sensitive period when the meetings were in session or the Party Congress was on, they would send people to escort Zhang Gang's parents on sightseeing excursions instead. Every year, the parents ended up enjoying the kind of expense account tourism that only Party leaders normally get to enjoy. After all this fruitless petitioning, their despair gave way to a taste for novelty, and every time a sensitive date approached, they would make a point of asking what famous scenic spot remained to be seen, meaning they would like to go and see it. The city government was at its wits' end—it was said that it must have spent a million yuan on Zhang Gang's parents during these ten years.

THE FIFTH DAY

I was searching for my father among the throngs of skeletal people. I had the uplifting sensation that he had left traces here, even if those traces were as faint as the distant call of a departing goose. Surely I would discern the marks he had left, just as one feels the movement of a breeze as it ruffles one's hair. I knew that I might not be able to recognize my father even if he was standing in front of me, but he would be able to recognize me at a glance. I would make my way toward the skeletal people—sometimes a large crowd, sometimes a small clump—and stand before them as though on display, hoping that one among them would call me by my name.

I knew that such a voice would sound foreign to my ears, just as Li Qing's greeting had sounded unfamiliar. But I would be able to distinguish my father's call just from his tone. In the world that had left me, there had always been an intimate note to my father's greeting, and in this new world that should remain unchanged.

Here there roamed everywhere the figures of those who had no graves. Denied a place of rest, these figures were like trees in motion—sometimes scattered, disconnected trees, sometimes dense stands of timber. When I walked among them, it was as though I were wending my way through a well-managed forest. I was looking forward to hearing the sound of my father's voice, ahead of me or behind me, to the left or the right. I was looking forward to that call of "Yang Fei!"

Often I would run into people wearing black armbands. With the black gauze fastened in place, their sleeves seemed empty. The absence of skin and flesh told me these people must have been here a long time. They would look at me and smile—a smile conveyed not by facial expression but through their vacant eyes. It was a smile of understanding, because we were all in the same boat. In the other world no one would wear a black armband on our behalf—we were all grieving for ourselves.

One such self-mourner noticed my searching look. He stood in front of me and I gazed at his bony face. There was a little hole in his forehead. He greeted me in a friendly fashion.

"Are you looking for someone?" he asked. "Or for several people?"

"Just one," I said. "My father. He may be here."

"Your father?"

"Yang Jinbiao is his name."

"Names don't mean anything here."

"He was in his sixties—"

"It's impossible to tell people's ages here."

I looked at the skeletons walking in the distance and close by, and it was true that one couldn't tell how old they were. My eyes could distinguish only tall and short, wide and narrow, and my ears could differentiate only male and female, old and young.

Recalling how debilitated my father had become in his final days, I added further details: "He's five foot seven, very thin—"

"Everyone here is thin."

Looking at these people who were all so thin that only their bones were left, I didn't know how further to describe my father.

"Do you remember what he was wearing when he came over?" he asked.

"A railroad uniform," I told him. "A brand-new railroad uniform."

"How long ago was it that he came over?"

"It's been over a year now."

"I've seen people in other kinds of uniform, but nobody wearing a railroad uniform."

"Maybe somebody else has noticed him."

"I've been here a long time. If I haven't seen him, nobody else will have, either."

"Maybe he changed his clothes."

"A lot of people do change before coming here, it's true."

"I feel he must be here somewhere."

"If you can't find him, he may have gone to the burial ground."

"He has no grave."

"If he has no grave, then he should be here."

As I wandered here and there in search of my father, I found myself once more approaching the two avid chess players. They sat cross-legged on the grass, as concentrated as two statues. Their bodies were completely motionless, and it was just their hands that continually gestured, as though making moves. I saw neither board nor chess pieces, just their hands moving forward and back or side to side, and I couldn't tell whether the game they were playing was Chinese chess or Go.

One skeleton's hand had just put down a piece, only to raise it again immediately. Two skeletal hands immediately clasped that skeletal hand, and their owner shouted, "You can't retract your move!"

The owner of the single hand cried out, "But you just retracted a move yourself."

"I retracted that move because you did that before."

"I did that because you retracted your previous move."

"I retracted that previous move because yesterday you retracted moves."

"Yesterday it was you who retracted a move first—that was why I did it."

"The day before yesterday it was you who started it."

"Well, who started it the day before that?"

The two of them kept up an endless wrangle, accusing each other of retracting moves and tracing their adversary's history of such misdeeds farther and farther back into the past, from days to months and from months to years.

"I can't let you take back that move," the owner of two of the hands cried. "I'm about to win."

"No, I'm taking back that move," the owner of the one hand cried.

"I'm not playing with you anymore."

"I'm not playing with you, either."

"I'm never going to play with you again."

"I've been wanting to stop playing with you for ages."

"Let me tell you something: I'm leaving. I'm going to get cremated tomorrow and then go off to my burial ground."

"I've been meaning to get cremated for ages now—can't wait to get to my burial ground!"

I interrupted their bickering. "I know your story."

"Everyone here knows our story," one of them said.

"Newcomers maybe don't," the other said.

"Even if they don't, our story is still kicking ass."

"Or, to put it more delicately, our story is the talk of the town."

"I know about your friendship too," I said.

"Friendship?"

The two of them chortled.

"What's friendship?" one asked the other.

"Haven't a clue," the other said.

Laughing away, they raised their heads, and two pairs of cavernous eyes looked at me. "You're a newbie, are you?" one of them asked.

"He came with that cute girl," the other said, before I had time to reply.

The two skeletons lowered their heads and with a titter resumed their game. It was as though they had never been arguing, as though neither of them had ever taken back a move.

After playing for a little while, one of them raised his head. "Do you know what board game we're playing?"

I glanced at the movements of their hands. "Chinese chess."

"Wrong. It's Go."

Soon the other one turned to me. "Now you know what we're playing, right?"

"Of course," I said. "You're playing Go."

"Wrong! It's Chinese chess."

They then asked me the following question at the same time: "Now what are we playing?"

"If it's not Go, it's got to be Chinese chess."

"Wrong again!" they said. "Now we're playing Five in a Row."

They heaved with laughter, each of them making exactly the same gestures, pressing one hand against his own midriff and the other hand on the other's shoulder. The two skeletons shook with laughter, like withered trees whose intersecting branches tremble together in the wind.

Afterward the two skeletons continued their game, but before long they were in an argument once more, because of yet another retracted move. It seemed to me that they were playing these games just in order to be able to argue, with each of them taking his turn to denounce the other's record of retracting moves. I stood there listening to the history of their happy chess playing and the history of their happy arguments. Gleefully each fulminated against the other's vile record of retracted moves, and when their respective surveys of past offenses finally went back as far as seven years earlier, I lost patience, knowing there were another seven or eight years of retracted moves still to be accounted for.

"Which of you is Zhang Gang?" I asked. I hesitated a moment, realizing suddenly the inappropriateness of referring to the other man as "the male surnamed Li," as the newspapers at the time put it. "And which of you is Mr. Li?"

"Mr. Li?"

They looked at each other, then burst into gales of laughter.

"Why don't you guess?" they both said.

I studied them carefully, and to me the two skeletons looked exactly alike. "I've no idea," I told them. "You could be twins, as far as I can tell."

"Twins?" Again they burst into laughter. Then, once more, they resumed their game in the most cordial of moods. The tempestuous argument of a moment earlier had vanished into thin air after my interruption.

Soon they were back to their old tricks, asking me, "Do you know what game we're playing?"

"Chinese chess, Go, Five in a Row." I recited all the possibilities.

"Wrong!" they chortled. "We're playing Chinese checkers."

Once again they burst out laughing and again I saw each of them gripping his midriff with one hand and clapping the other hand on his adversary's shoulder. The two skeletons shook with a tidy rhythm.

I laughed too. More than ten years ago, the two of them had come here, six months apart. The grudge between them had not crossed the frontier between life and death. Enmity had been sealed off in that departed world.

My search continued endlessly, like the hands on a clock that go round and round but can never leave the dial. My father was nowhere to be found.

Several times I ran into a crowd of skeletons, dozens of them. They were not like the other skeletons that sometimes gathered together and sometimes separated—this crowd stayed consistently together as they walked, a little like the moon's reflection on water, which keeps floating in a discrete shape no matter how the waves tug.

The fourth time I ran into this bunch, I came to a halt and so did they. We sized each other up. Their hands were linked and their bodies leaned on each other, and they grouped together like a flourishing tree whose branches spread high and low. I knew that among them there were men and women, old and young. I smiled and greeted them.

"Hello!" they responded in unison, a chorus of male and female voices, hoarse old voices and tender young voices, and I saw a cheerful outlook in their empty eyes.

"How many of you are there?" I asked.

"Thirty-eight," they answered.

"Why are you always together?"

"We arrived at the same time," a man's voice answered.

"We're all one family," a woman's voice added.

Then I heard a boy's voice. "Why are you on your own?"

"I'm not entirely on my own." I looked down at the black armband on my left arm. "I'm looking for my father. He's wearing a railroad uniform."

Another voice piped up from among the skeletons in front of me. "We haven't seen anyone in a railroad uniform."

"He may have changed his clothes before coming here," I said.

The crisp voice of a little girl rang out. "Daddy, is he new here?"

"Yes," the male voices said.

"Mom, is he new here?"

"That's right," the female voices said.

"Are they all your moms and dads?" I asked the little girl.

"That's right," she said. "In the past I just had one mom and one dad, but now I've got lots of moms and lots of dads."

"How did you get here?" the boy who'd addressed me earlier asked.

"I think it was a fire," I said.

"How come he's not burned?" he asked the skeletons next to him.

I could feel their silent, rapt gaze. "After I saw the fire," I told them, "I heard an explosion and the building must have collapsed."

"Were you crushed to death?" the little girl asked.

"I think that's maybe what happened, yes."

"His face has been altered," the little boy said.

"You're right."

"Are we pretty?" the little girl asked.

I looked awkwardly at the thirty-eight skeletons arrayed in front of me, unsure how to respond to the girl's blunt inquiry.

"Everyone here says I keep getting prettier," the little girl said.

"That's true," the boy said. "They say everyone who comes here just gets uglier, and we're the only ones who get prettier."

I hesitated for a moment. "I wouldn't know," I answered in the end.

The voice of an elderly person sounded among them. "We were so charred in the fire that when we got here we were like thirty-eight knots of charcoal. Later, the burned bits peeled off, leaving us as we are now. That's why people say this."

He recounted their story as the other thirty-seven listened silently. Now I knew their history, how, on the day of my father's disappearance, that department store half a mile from my little shop caught on fire and was reduced to a pile of blackened ruins. The city government had reported that seven had died and twenty-one were injured, of whom two were in critical condition. On the Internet some said over fifty had perished, and some even claimed the death toll topped one hundred. I looked at the thirty-eight skeletons in front of me: they were the deleted dead. But what about their relatives?

"Why did your families not make a fuss?"

"They received threats, and they accepted hush money as well," the old one answered. "We're already dead, and just so long as our relatives can go on living an undisturbed life, we'll be content."

"But the children? Won't their parents—"

"We're the kids' parents now," the old man interrupted me.

Holding hands, one next to the other, they silently slipped past me and went on their way. They moved on in a tight throng, and even the strongest wind could not have blown them apart.

In the far distance I spotted a couple, still fully fleshed, emerging from a lush stand of mulberry trees. They were dressed very skimpily, in garments that looked more like simple coverings than real apparel. As they came nearer, I realized that the woman was dressed in only a black bra and panties and the man in blue underpants. The woman wore a shocked expression and walked with a slight crouch, her hands folded across her thighs as if to screen them from view. The man bent down and put his arm around her protectively.

As they arrived in front of me, they scanned me carefully, as though searching for a familiar face. Disappointment gradually registered on their features, for they had decided they did not recognize me.

"Are you a new arrival?" the man asked.

I nodded. "And you are, too? Husband and wife, I take it?"

They nodded simultaneously.

"Did you see our daughter?" the woman asked pathetically.

I shook my head. "There's such a multitude of people over there," I said, "I don't know which of them is your daughter."

The woman bowed her head in distress. The man patted her on the shoulder. "There will be other new arrivals," he comforted her.

"Yes, but there's such a multitude of people over there," the woman answered, repeating what I'd just said.

"There's bound to be someone who has seen Xiaomin," the man said.

Xiaomin? I seemed to have heard this name before. "How did you come to be here?" I asked.

A wisp of fear crossed their faces as the shadow of their ordeal in that departed world projected into this one. Their eyes evaded my glance—or perhaps it was their tears that made them appear to do so.

Then the man began to recount their terrifying experience that morning on Amity Street. The city had been determined to demolish the three apartment buildings, but the residents had refused to move out, resisting all pressure for a good three months, until forcible demolition was authorized. The couple came home early one morning after getting off the night shift, woke up their daughter, and prepared breakfast for her. She went off to school, her satchel on her back, while they went to bed and fell asleep. In their dreams they heard a loudspeaker outside delivering one warning after another, but they were just too tired to wake up properly. In the past they had heard other such warnings and seen bulldozers lined up in combat readiness, but after the confrontation with the residents, the loudspeakers and bulldozers had retreated. So they thought this was simply another round of intimidation and went on sleeping. They were shaken awake only when the building began to sway violently amid a clamorous din. The man jumped out of bed, tugging his wife by the hand, and ran toward the door. Just as he opened it, she ran over to the sofa to collect her jacket. He dashed back to pull her away—and the building collapsed with a crash.

His account came to an abrupt halt, and she began to weep.

"I'm sorry, I'm so sorry—"

"Don't say that."

"I shouldn't have tried to get my jacket—"

"We didn't have enough time anyway. Even if you hadn't gone back, we wouldn't have had time to escape."

"If I hadn't tried to pick up the jacket, you would have got out alive."

"Even if I'd got out, where would that have left you?"

"Well, at least Xiaomin would have a father."

I realized now who their daughter was—the little girl in the red down jacket who sat amid the chaos of steel and concrete, doing her homework in the cold wind as she waited for her parents to come home.

"I've seen your daughter," I told them. "Her name is Zheng Xiaomin."

"Yes!" they cried together. "That's her name."

"She's in fourth grade."

"That's right. How do you know?" they asked.

"We've talked on the phone," I told the man. "I'm the one who promised to do the tutoring."

"You're Teacher Yang?"

"Yes, I'm Yang Fei."

The man turned to the woman. "This is Teacher Yang. I told him we didn't make much money and he immediately lowered his fee to thirty yuan an hour."

"That was kind of you," the woman said.

To hear thanks in this context made me smile wanly.

"How is it you're here too?" the man asked.

"I was sitting in a restaurant when the kitchen caught fire, and then there was an explosion. I arrived on the same day as you, just a few hours later. I called you from the restaurant, but you didn't pick up."

"I didn't hear the phone ring."

"You were buried in the ruins then."

"You're right." The man looked at his wife. "The phone was probably crushed."

"How was Xiaomin?" she asked impatiently.

"We had arranged that I would come to your apartment at four p.m. When I got there, the three buildings were no longer standing. . . ."

I hesitated for a moment, and decided not to tell them

how their deaths had been hushed up. A story would be concocted about how the two of them had died. Their daughter would receive an urn in which other people's ashes had been placed, and would grow up believing in a beautiful lie.

"How is Xiaomin?" the woman asked again.

"She's well," I said. "She's the most levelheaded girl I've ever met. You don't need to worry about her. She knows how to take care of herself."

"She's only eleven," the girl's mother moaned. "Every time she leaves the house to go to school, she'll stop after a few yards and call, 'Dad,' and 'Mom,' and wait for us to respond. Then she'll say, 'I'm off now,' and head off to school."

"What did she tell you?" the father asked.

I remembered how she told me she was cold and how I suggested she do her homework in the KFC nearby and how she shook her head, saying that her mom and dad wouldn't know where she was when they came home.

After hesitating once more, I decided I should tell these things to her parents, adding, "She was sitting right above you."

Tears flowed silently down their faces, and I knew that theirs was a wellspring of grief that would never dry. My eyes misted up too as I went on my way. After I had gone some distance, the wailing behind me pursued me like a tidal surge. Just the two of them wept as much as a whole crowd might. In my mind's eye the tide carried the girl in the red down jacket and tossed her onto a beach, and when the waters retreated she was left all alone, there in the human world.

⋅ᚗ

I saw what a feast was like here. In a land of scented grasses and babbling streams, there were thriving vegetables and

143

trees laden with fruit. The dead sat around in circles on the grass, as though seated around the multiple tables of a banquet hall. Their movements were infinitely varied: some ate rapidly and with great determination, some savored things slowly, some chatted away, some smoked and drank, some raised glasses in a toast, some rubbed their bellies when full. . . . I saw several people with flesh and others just with bones shuttling back and forth, and they were making the motions of carrying dishes and pouring wine, so I knew these were serving staff.

When I approached, a skeleton greeted me. "Welcome to the Tan Family Eatery."

This name, rendered in a young woman's dulcet tones, gave me a start. Then I heard an unfamiliar voice call my name: "Yang Fei."

I turned my head and there was Tan Jiaxin making his way toward me with a limp. His right hand looked as though a plate rested on top of it. I saw a happy expression on his face, an expression I had never seen in that departed world, where his smile had always been forced.

He came up to me. "Yang Fei, when did you get here?"

"Yesterday."

"We've been here four days."

As he spoke, he held up his right hand as though carrying a dish. He turned around and called his wife and daughter, and then his son-in-law, conveying his happiness to them. "Yang Fei's here!"

Soon the rest of the family came over, all holding plates and carrying bottles. Tan Jiaxin hailed them as they approached. "Yang Fei made it for the opening."

They came to me and looked me up and down, beaming and chuckling. "You look thinner," Tan Jiaxin's wife said.

"We're thinner, too," Tan said cheerfully. "Everyone who

comes here is bound to lose some weight. Everyone here has a fine figure."

"How come you're here too?" his daughter asked.

"I have no burial plot. How about you?"

Tan's face darkened. "Our relatives are all in Guangdong," he said. "They maybe don't know what happened to us."

"But the four of us are all here," Tan's wife pointed out.

A happy expression returned to Tan's face. "That's right," he said. "Our family's all together."

"You broke your leg?" I asked.

"With a broken leg I can walk all the more quickly." He gave a ringing laugh.

A cry rose up from one of the groups of diners. "Hey, what about our dishes? And our drinks?"

Tan turned and responded with a shout. "Be right there!"

He moved off quickly, limping heavily, his right hand appearing to hold a plate. His wife, daughter, and son-in-law rushed off to attend to the diners, looking as though they were holding plates and carrying bottles of spirits.

Tan Jiaxin looked back over his shoulder. "What will you have?"

"The usual bowl of noodles," I said.

"You got it."

I found a place, and when I sat down on the grass I felt as though I were sitting on a chair. Opposite me sat a skeleton, and his only gesture was that of putting a glass to his lips, with no effort to pick up food with chopsticks and put things in his mouth. His vacant eyes gazed at the black armband on my arm.

His outfit looked strange to me. His black clothes hung very loosely, but they lacked sleeves, revealing the skeleton's arms and shoulders, and their dark color seemed to indicate they had undergone months and years of exposure to the elements. There was a raw edge where the shoulders of his garment would have met the arms; it looked as though the sleeves had been torn off.

We looked at each other. He was the first to speak. "What day did you come over?"

"It's my fifth day," I said. "I got here yesterday."

He raised his glass and gulped down the contents. Then he set his glass on the ground and went through the motions of refilling it. "All on your own, I see." He sighed.

I bowed my head in acknowledgment, glancing at the black gauze on my arm.

"At least you knew to wear an armband for yourself," he said. "Some lonely madcaps arrive here without any armband, and they get so envious when they see others with them that they come and hassle me to tear off a piece of sleeve."

I looked at the skeletal arm and shoulder that were exposed to view and couldn't help but smile.

He made a gesture of raising his glass, downing the shot, and setting the glass back on the ground. "The sleeves were very long originally, reaching below my fingers. But now look at them—both shoulders are exposed." He used his hands to make his point.

"What about you?" I asked. "You don't need an armband?"

"I've got family over there," he said. "But they've maybe forgotten me."

He went through the motions of picking up the bottle and refilling his glass, indicating through the movement that it was his last glass, and once more he made the gesture of swallowing the contents in one draft.

"That's good stuff," he said.

"What are you drinking?" I asked.

"Rice wine."

"What brand?"

"I don't know."

I smiled. "How long have you been here?"

"I've forgotten."

"It has to be a long time, then."

"Too long."

"You must have seen a lot during your time here, so there's something I'd like to ask you." I shared with him a thought that had suddenly occurred to me. "How do I get the feeling that after death there's actually eternal life?"

He looked at me with his empty eyes but said nothing.

"Why is it that after death one needs to go to the place of rest?"

He seemed to smile. "I don't know."

"I don't understand why you need to bake yourself into a little box of ashes."

"That's the custom," he said.

"If you have a grave, you have a resting place, and if you don't have a grave, you gain eternal life—which do you think is better?"

"I don't know," he said once more.

Then he turned his head and called, "Waitress, the check."

A skeleton waitress walked over. "Fifty yuan."

He made a gesture of placing fifty yuan on the table, then got to his feet, nodding to me. "Young fellow, don't think so much," he murmured as he left.

I looked at his loose black clothes and his skeletal arms, and couldn't help but think of a beetle. His silhouette gradually got smaller until it disappeared among the other skeletons.

Tan Jiaxin's son-in-law came over, making the motion of holding a bowl of noodles in both hands, followed by the motion of giving it to me, and my hands made the gestures of accepting it from him.

When I made the gesture of placing the bowl of noodles on the ground, it felt as though I were placing it on a table. Then my left hand made the gesture of holding the bowl and my right hand made the gesture of holding chopsticks. I completed the motion of taking a mouthful of noodles and my mouth began the motion of tasting them. To me they tasted the same as noodles in the departed world.

I became aware that all around me was laughter and good cheer, as people tucked into their meals and exchanged toasts, at the same time gleefully mocking those defective food items so pervasive in the departed world: tainted rice, tainted milk formula, tainted buns, fake eggs, leather milk, plaster noodles, chemical hot pot, fecal tofu, ersatz chili powder, recycled cooking oil.

Amid hoots of laughter, they sang the praises of the dishes here, and I heard words such as "fresh," "delicious," and "healthy" being bandied about.

"There are only two places we know where food is safe," someone said.

"Which two places?"

"Here is one."

"What about the other?"

"The state banquets over there."

"Well said," someone chuckled. "We're enjoying the same treatment as those top leaders."

As I smiled I noticed that I was no longer making the motion of eating noodles and realized that I had finished.

"Check, please!" someone next to me called.

A skeletal waitress came over. "Eighty-seven yuan," she said.

"Here's a hundred."

"Thirteen yuan change," the waitress said.

"Thanks," the diner said.

Paying the bill was simply an exchange of words, with no action involved. At this point Tan Jiaxin came limping over, making the gesture of holding a dish in his palm. I knew he was giving me a fruit plate, so I made the gesture of taking it from him. He sat down opposite me. "Fresh fruit, just picked," he said.

I began the motion of eating fruit and tasted sweet, delicious flavors. "The Tan Family Eatery didn't need long to get going," I said.

"There's no public security bureau, fire department, or sanitation, commerce, or tax department here," he said. "To open a restaurant over there, the fire department will hold things back for a year or two, claiming that your restaurant poses a fire risk, and the sanitation department will delay things for a year or two on the grounds that your sanitation level is not up to standard. You have to give them money and gifts before they will grant you a permit."

An uneasy look then crossed his face. "You're not angry with us, are you?"

"Why would I be angry?"

"You were stuck in the room."

I recalled the last scene in that world, of Tan Jiaxin gazing at me through the smoke and shouting to me.

"You seemed to be shouting," I said.

"I was telling you to run." He sighed. "We didn't manage to hold anybody back, only you."

I shook my head. "It wasn't that you held me back—I just didn't leave."

I didn't tell him about the newspaper and the report on Li Qing's suicide, for that would be too long a story. Maybe on some other occasion I would take him through it all, slowly.

Tan Jiaxin was still struggling with an uneasy conscience. He explained why, after the kitchen fire began, they had to block the front door and try to have the customers pay before leaving. The restaurant had been operating in the red for three years in a row.

"I must have been crazy," he said. "I ruined myself, I ruined my family, and I ruined you."

"Coming here is not so bad," I said. "My dad's here too."

"Your dad's here?" Tan Jiaxin was pleased. "Why didn't you come together?"

"I haven't found him yet," I said. "But I have the feeling he's not far away."

"Once you find him, be sure to bring him here," Tan Jiaxin said.

"I'll be sure to do that," I said.

Tan Jiaxin sat down opposite me, no longer with a frown on his face but wreathed in smiles. As he got up to leave, he urged me once more to bring my father to taste their dishes.

Then I settled my bill. A skeletal girl came over—a new hire, I assumed. "The noodles are eleven yuan," she said. "The fruit is complimentary."

"Here's twenty," I said.

"Here's your change," she said.

Again, an exchange of words was all that was involved. As I turned to leave, this skeletal girl called to me warmly, "Good to see you! Please come again!"

◆◇

In front of a verdant bamboo grove, a skeleton wearing a black armband came over to me. I noticed a little hole in his forehead and realized that I'd seen him before. I smiled at him and he smiled too. His smile was not a mobile expression of feeling as much as a light breeze wafting from his vacant eyes and empty mouth.

"There's a bonfire over there," he said. "See, over there."

I looked into the far distance, in the direction of his outstretched finger. A broad meadow spread almost as far as the eye could see, and where the meadow ended there was something bright and glistening, like a silk sash—it looked to me like a river. A green fire was blazing far off in the distance, like the little flame that burns when one flicks on a cigarette lighter. Skeletal people were coming down the hillside and out of the woods, and I could see a number of little groups heading toward the fire.

"How about we go over and join them?" he suggested.

"What's going on there?" I asked.

"There's a bonfire by the river," he said.

"Do they often go there?"

"Not often, but every now and then."

"Everyone here goes?"

"No." He glanced at my armband and pointed at his own. "Just people like us."

I understood now. Over there was where self-mourners would congregate. I nodded and followed him toward the bonfire and the silk-sash river. The grass whispered as we wended our way.

I looked at his black armband. "How do you come to be here?" I asked.

"Oh, it's a long story," he said.

A note of remembrance appeared in his voice. "I'd been married a couple of years then. My wife had a mental illness, but I didn't realize that before we married, because I had met her only three times. I did sense something a bit odd about her smile, and it made me feel a little uneasy. But my parents weren't at all concerned, and her family circumstances were good, with a large dowry and twenty thousand yuan in the bank. The village where I'm from is very poor, and it's parents who make decisions when it comes to choosing a marriage partner. With that kind of money you can build a two-story house. So my parents went ahead with the match, and it was only later that it became clear she was mentally disturbed.

"She wasn't that terrible—she didn't hit me or make a fuss—but she'd spend the whole day laughing at this and that and got absolutely nothing done. My parents regretted their decision and felt they'd let me down, but they wouldn't let me get a divorce, saying that the house had already been built and it wouldn't do to dump her after profiting from her wealth. I hadn't been thinking of divorce, either, and preferred just to carry on as we were doing. She was gentle and quiet as mental cases go, sleeping peacefully at night like any normal person.

"One summer day she went off by herself—I don't think she had any idea where she was going. I went out to look for her, and so did my parents and my brother and sister-in-law. We looked all over the place and made inquiries everywhere, but could find no trace of her. After three days of futile searching, we went to tell her family. They jumped to the conclusion that I must have murdered her, and they went to the local public security bureau to report their suspicions.

"Five days after she left home, a woman's body floated to the surface of a pond a mile from our village. It being the height of summer, the corpse was already decomposed and unrecognizable. The police called me and my wife's relatives in to try to make an identification, but none of us could be sure, at most simply noting a similarity in heights. The police said the drowning happened on the day she left home, and to me this suggested strongly that it must be my wife, and her family felt the same. She must have stumbled carelessly into the pond, I thought, for she wouldn't have realized the danger of drowning. It upset me, for whatever else you say about it, we had been husband and wife for over two years.

"A couple of days later, the policemen came back to ask what I was doing the day my wife left. I'd gone into town that morning and it was evening when I got home and discovered she was gone. The police asked if anyone could testify that I had gone into town. I thought that over and said no. They took notes and left. Her family was convinced I had killed her and the police thought so too, so they arrested me.

"At the outset, my parents and my brother and his wife didn't believe I killed her, but later, when I admitted I had, they were finally convinced. They were very upset and hated me for shaming them so much—they couldn't raise their heads. That's what our village is like: if there's a murderer in the family, nobody dares to venture out of the house. When the court sentenced me to death not one of them was in attendance, and it was only her family who came. I don't bear them any grudge. After I was arrested, they wanted to visit me but the police wouldn't let them. They're all honest, simple people, and they had no idea I was unjustly accused.

"I had no choice but to say I'd done it. The police strung me up and beat me, insisting I confess, beating me till I was shitting and pissing in my pants. My hands were tied tightly for two whole days and four of my fingers went black—I'd never be able to use them again, I was told. Later, they strung me up by my feet instead, with my head pointing down. When you get beaten that way, it's not your body that hurts most, but your eyes. Tears are salty, and they can be as painful as a needle stabbing you in the eyes. I thought I'd be better off dead, so I admitted the crime."

He paused for a moment. "You know why we have eyebrows?"

"Why?"

"To block sweat."

I heard him chuckle as he smiled to himself.

He pointed at the back of his head, then at the round hole in his forehead. "The bullet came in the back, and this is where it came out."

He looked down at his black armband. "When I got here, I noticed that some people were wearing armbands for themselves, and I wanted to do the same. I felt nobody back there would wear an armband for me—certainly nobody in my family. I saw someone with a long, loose black jacket. I asked him if he would mind tearing off a piece of sleeve for me. He understood what I had in mind, and complied. With a black armband I feel at ease.

"Someone who came over later filled me in on what happened subsequently. Six months after I was shot, my wife suddenly returned home. Her clothes were ragged and torn, and her face was so filthy nobody could recognize her. She stood outside the front door cackling happily away, and eventually someone put two and two together.

"Everyone finally realized that I had been wrongly convicted. My parents and my brother and sister-in-law all wept for two days straight, so upset were they. The government gave them compensation to the tune of five hundred thousand yuan, and they bought a fine grave for me—"

"You have a burial site?" I asked. "Why are you still here?"

"At first, when I heard the news, I took off my armband and tossed it under a tree, preparing to head there straightaway. But before I'd gone ten yards, I felt I couldn't bear to leave here, so I went back and put the armband on again. Now I don't feel like going."

"You don't want to go to the place of rest?"

"No, I do," he said. "My thought at the time was that I have a burial spot all lined up, so there's no big hurry—I can go there whenever I feel like it."

"How long have you been here?"

"Eight years now."

"Is the burial plot still there?"

"Yes, it always has been."

"When do you plan to go?"

"Sometime in the future."

We walked to the gathering place of the self-mourners. Before my eyes there stretched a broad river—the gleaming scene had also broadened. A green bonfire was blazing vigorously on the riverbank, and the leaping sparks looked like dancing glowworms.

Already there were many skeletons wearing armbands sitting around the bonfire. I followed my companion into the throng, looking for a spot to sit. Some of those seated adjusted their positions, opening up several vacant spots. I stood there in a quandary, until I saw my new friend sitting down in a nearby spot; I sat down next to him. When I raised my head, I saw others approaching, some along the grassy hills, some along the riverbank; they were blending together the way quiet little streams spill into a wider flow.

The skeleton next to me gave a friendly greeting. "Hi there!"

"Hi there!" seemed to form a little soundwave, veering off, making a circuit around the bonfire, then returning to me before it subsided completely.

"Are they greeting me?" I whispered.

"That's right," he said. "You're a new arrival."

I felt that I was a tree transplanted back to its native forest, a drop of water returning to the river, a mote of dust returning to the earth.

One by one the armband-wearing self-mourners sat down, and voices gradually reverted to quiescence. We sat around the bonfire, and in the spacious silence there quietly surged a thousand words and ten thousand comments—the sound of many humble lives presenting an account of themselves. Every one of the self-mourners had bitter memories, too painful to recall, of that departed world; every one was a lonely orphan there. Mourning ourselves, we gathered here, but when we sat in a circle around the green bonfire, we were no longer lonely and abandoned.

There was no talking, no movement, just silent, understanding smiles. We sat in the silence, not with any goal in mind, just for the sensation that we were united, instead of being isolated individuals.

In the quiet circle of sitters I heard the dancing of the fire, the tapping of the water, the swaying of the grass, the soughing of the trees, the rustling of the breeze, the floating of the clouds.

These sounds seemed to be pouring out their woes, as though they too had suffered many reverses, ordeals too painful to recall. Then I heard snatches of a song reaching me, a song like that of the nightingale. I would hear a little burst of song, and then a pause, and then another burst of song. . . .

I heard a sound like a whisper in my ear. "So, you're here."

When I walked toward this unfamiliar voice, it was like

raindrops dripping from the eaves onto a windowsill, clear and light. I could tell that it was a woman's voice, one that after enduring hardship and heartache had been reduced to twilight's dim glow, but still retained a distinct rhythm, like a knock on the door—one, two, three. "So, you're here."

I was a bit confused. Was this greeting really directed at me? But there was a faraway intimacy—the kind of intimacy you find in the depths of memory—that made me feel this greeting was for me. It was followed by a song like that of the nightingale, rippling toward me, and then that tender greeting reached my ears once more.

I walked toward the warbling song, toward the call of "So, you're here."

I entered a copse of trees, and it seemed to me that the nightingale-like song was gliding down from the trees in front of me. As I came closer, I noticed that the tree leaves were getting bigger and bigger, and then I saw a line of tiny skeletal babies settled in the cradles formed by the spreading, swaying leaves, and the babies were rocking back and forth and singing a song that tugged at the heartstrings. I stretched out my fingers and counted them one by one, until I reached twenty-seven. This number made my heart quiver, and my memory at once caught up with that lost world, and I thought of those twenty-seven dead babies labeled "medical refuse" that were washed up on the riverbank.

"So, you're here."

I saw a skeleton dressed in bright white clothing sitting in the tall grass between the trees. She stood up slowly, gave a sigh, and said to me, "Son, how did you come to be here so soon?"

I knew who she was. "Mom," I called softly.

Li Yuezhen walked up to me. Her empty eyes gazed at me

and her voice sounded uncertain. "You look to be in your fifties, but you're only forty-one."

"You still remember my age," I said.

"You're the same age as Hao Xia," she said.

By this time Hao Xia and Hao Qiangsheng were in America, in that other world, while Li Yuezhen and I were here in this one. When they left, I saw them off at the airport; they were flying to Shanghai and then taking a connecting flight from there. I asked Hao Qiangsheng to let me carry the urn of ashes, so that I could accompany this spiritual mother of mine for a small portion of her final journey.

"I saw you carrying the urn to the airport." Li Yuezhen shook her head. "But they weren't my ashes, they were someone else's."

Those ashes, I realized, must now be resting under her name, somewhere in America. "Hao Xia told she has already found a resting place for you," I started to say, "and her dad will join you there in the future."

I didn't go on, because I realized now that when Hao Qiangsheng was buried his remains would not be interred with those of Li Yuezhen, but with those of one or more strangers.

Tears streamed from Li Yuezhen's empty eyes, for this thought had occurred to her too. Tears flowed down her stonelike cheeks and fell onto the blades of grass below. Then her empty eyes lit up with a happier expression, and she raised her head to look at the warbling babies. "I used to have twenty-seven children. Now that you're here, I've got twenty-eight."

Her fingers, reduced simply to bones, began to stroke the black armband on my left arm. She knew that I was grieving for myself. "My poor boy," she said.

In my ice-bound heart there appeared a warming glow. One of the infants, overreaching, tumbled down off a leaf and, sobbing pitifully, crawled over Li Yuezhen. She took the infant into her arms and gently rocked him back and forth, then set him back on top of another broad leaf, where he happily rejoined the warbling chorus.

"How did you get here?" Li Yuezhen asked.

I told her about my final moments, and also mentioned how Li Qing had come from so far away to say goodbye.

She gave a sigh. "Li Qing should never have left you."

Perhaps she was right, I thought. If Li Qing had not left me at that point, we might still be living a peaceful life in that other world and our child would be in primary school—or maybe even middle school.

I recalled the disappearance of Li Yuezhen and the dead babies and how the funeral parlor had claimed that it had already cremated them all, though it was said that their ashes had actually been taken from the urns of other people altogether.

"I know about that," she said. "People who came after me told me."

I looked up at the babies singing away on the broad tree leaves. "Did you carry them all here?"

"No, I didn't carry them," she said. "I walked in front and they crawled along behind."

Li Yuezhen said that late that night she did not hear the roar of the subsidence. She had been sleeping heavily, and at one stage she saw a vast chaos in which heaven and earth were inextricably mixed. A gleam of light appeared in the far distance, like a line on the horizon, and then light came rolling in like a tide. Heaven and earth separated, morning and night were uncoupled. Later, in her dreams she felt air whirling around rapidly and shuttling back and forth, and in the final stage of sleep she saw water spreading from the ground and rising inexorably until it was like an ocean.

Then she woke, to find she seemed to be falling vertically off a cliff. She slowly pushed aside the white cloth, the way she might sweep away snow in front of her door. Her feet began to move, taking her out of the morgue that now lay at the bottom of the sinkhole, bathed in a desolate moonlight. Her feet stepped on a broken wall as jagged as scattered dogs' teeth, and she propelled herself out of the pit.

She walked into a city flooded with light, where pedestrians and cars jostled. Everything was the same as it had always been, but departure into another realm put her beyond the reach of this familiar world.

Out of habit she walked to the building where she used to live, as though returning home, but she could not enter it as she would have been able to before. No matter how she moved her legs, it was impossible to get closer. Three days after her departure from the human world, she saw a female figure appear briefly at a sixth-floor window and her heart skipped a beat, for it was Hao Xia—her daughter had returned.

In the two days and nights that followed, she never ceased in her efforts to approach the building, but she just seemed to move farther away. Hao Qiangsheng never appeared in that window and neither did I, and Hao Xia appeared just that once. She saw people moving tables and chairs and chests out of the building, then coffee tables and sofas and beds, until she knew that the furniture she had lived with for decades had been sold off and the apartment itself too, for her husband and daughter were about to fly to America.

Finally, one afternoon, she saw all three of us. Hao Qiangsheng, holding an urn in both hands, emerged from the building; he was supported by Hao Xia, who held in her right hand a large duffel bag, while I followed behind carrying a large suitcase in each hand. The three of us stood by the side of the road and a taxi pulled over. The driver and I together put the bag and suitcases into the trunk of the car. She saw me say a few words to Hao Qiangsheng, and he passed the urn to me. Holding it carefully in both hands, I sat down in the passenger seat, while Hao Xia and her father sat in the back. The taxi drove off.

She knew that this was a final parting, for her husband and daughter were leaving for far-off America. Tears came to her eyes and she dashed forward to deliver a greeting, but running simply put more distance between her and us. She came to a halt and watched as the the taxi disappeared in the flow of traffic.

She started sobbing then, and after much grieving she heard behind her a murmur, a murmur a bit like a sob, and when she turned around she saw the twenty-seven babies crawling along the ground in a line. At first they appeared to be just as upset as she was, but when her crying stopped, their susurrant sobs ceased too. She had not realized that they'd followed her out of the sinkhole and crawled all the way here. She gazed at the city that was gradually fading into the distance, then looked back at the twenty-seven babies, and realized what she had lost and what she had gained.

"Let's go," she said softly to the babies.

Li Yuezhen, dressed in white, walked forward slowly and the twenty-seven babies crawled after her all in a line. The sunlight was a grubby yellow as they threaded their way through the noisy city and entered a quiet space where they were greeted by silvery moonlight. They penetrated deeper and deeper into the silence.

After crossing the frontier between life and death, Li

Yuezhen stepped onto a stretch of fragrant grass. The green grass rubbed the necks of the twenty-seven babies crawling along behind, and the ticklish sensation made them giggle. Where the grass ended, a gleaming river flowed. Li Yuezhen waded into the river, which slowly rose to the level of her chest, then slowly fell until it lay beneath her feet, as she arrived at the other bank. The babies paddled on the surface of the water, spluttering as they made the crossing, the sound of their little coughs carrying to her until they reached the bank. As they entered a forest, Li Yuezhen began to sing a song, and the babies behind sang along with her. She stopped, but they did not, and their nightingale-like refrain continued to waft among the trees.

"Your father was here," Li Yuezhen said to me. "Yang Jinbiao was here."

I looked at her in wonder.

"He had to travel a long road to get here, so he was very tired," she said. "He lay down here for several days, thinking of you the whole time."

"Where did he go after leaving me?"

"He got on the train and went to the place where he once abandoned you."

That last evening's conversation with my father had always been imprinted on my mind. We squeezed onto the narrow little bed in the room behind the shop, and the streetlights outside seemed ready to drift off to sleep as the night breeze caressed our window. It was the first time my father had wept in front of me. He told me how, for a young woman's sake, he had abandoned me on a rock in an unfamiliar town. He described the rough texture of the rock face and the smoothness of its upper surface. It was on that terrace that he had put me, although subsequently he would reproach himself for his heartlessness, over and over again. When my father left me after that conversation more than a year ago, it never crossed my mind that this was where he would go.

My father had put on his brand-new railroad uniform, the newest set of clothes in his possession, which he'd never been able to bring himself to wear before. Dragging a weak and failing body, he boarded the train and squeezed his way to his seat. No sooner had he sat down than the train started to move. Watching the platform slowly recede into the distance, he suddenly became aware that he did not have much time left and did not know if he would ever be able to see me again.

My father told Li Yuezhen that he had not slept a wink that last night we were together, but instead listened continuously to my rhythmic breathing and occasional snoring. In the middle of the night there was a spell when I made no sound at all and he got worried, so he stretched out a hand and patted my face and neck, waking me. I propped myself up and looked at him, and he closed his eyes and pretended to be asleep. He said that in the darkness I patted him and carefully put his arm inside the quilt.

I shook my head. "I don't remember any of that," I told Li Yuezhen.

Li Yuezhen pointed at the grassy patch under the trees. "He was lying just there as he told me all this."

My father had a fairly clear idea of where to go, but it wasn't easy to find the copse of trees and the dark rock, and he never found the stone-slab bridge and the dry riverbed. He remembered that on the opposite side of the bridge there ought to be a building, a building with the sound of children singing, but he found neither the building nor the singing. Everything had changed, he told Li Yuezhen, even the train. The train that he and I took that year had pulled out of the platform at dawn and did not arrive at the town until midday. Now the train that he alone took still left at dawn, but reached that same place just over an hour later.

"Did you still remember the location?" Li Yuezhen asked him.

"I did," he said. "Riverside Street."

He left the train station in the morning sunlight, among travelers who carried bags over their shoulders or pulled suitcases behind them in such a rush it was as though their lives depended on it. He was carrying neither bag nor suitcase, but his laboring body felt heavier than any piece of luggage. As he plodded slowly toward the station exit, his two hands lacked the energy to swing loose and hung almost motionless by his side.

He stood in the square in front of the station and in a feeble voice asked directions from the healthy bodies rushing past him. Of the first twenty people he approached, only four said they were locals. He asked them how to get to Riverside Street. The three younger people had no idea where Riverside Street was. But the fourth, an old man, recognized the name and said my father needed to take a No. 3 bus. My father wearily boarded the bus, and in a town where he knew no one he went looking for the site of my abandonment.

"Why did you want to go there?" Li Yuezhen asked him.

"I just wanted to sit on that rock for a bit," he replied.

It was afternoon by the time he found the spot. He was well-nigh exhausted by the trip on crowded public transport. After he got off the first bus, he had sat down by the side of the road for a good long time before he could summon the strength to board the second. The third bus dropped him off three hundred yards from Riverside Street. To him, that walk was so arduous, it could just as well have been three thousand yards. He could move forward only with difficulty, his steps ponderous, his feet as heavy and clumsy as two rocks. After walking five or six yards, he had to lean against a tree to rest for a little. He noticed a snack shop by the side of the road and felt he ought to eat something, so he sat down on one of the stools placed on the sidewalk outside the shop, propping himself up by putting both hands on the table. He ordered a bowl of dumpling soup, but after three mouthfuls he had to throw up—into a plastic bag he had brought along for the purpose. The people sitting next to him hurriedly carried their bowls into the shop, and he apologized to them in a weak voice, then went on eating, continuing to vomit at intervals. When he finished eating, he felt he'd eaten more than he'd vomited and his body now had some strength, so he lurched to his feet and tottered the rest of the way to Riverside Street.

"It was all tall buildings there," he told Li Yuezhen.

The stream and the stone-slab bridge of yesteryear were no more. He did hear children, but they were no longer singing. They were yelling with excitement on a playground slide, as their watchful grandparents chatted. The area was now a housing complex, and the pathways between the high-rise buildings were like narrow cracks through which vehicles and people had to squeeze. He inquired as to the whereabouts of the river and the bridge, but the residents had all moved here from somewhere else, and according to them there was no river and no bridge, and there never had been. "Is this Riverside Street?" he asked, and they said it was. "Was that always its name?" he asked, and they said they thought it was.

"So it was called Riverside Street, even if there was no river?" Li Yuezhen asked.

"The place name hadn't changed, but everything else had," he replied.

In a feeble voice my father continued to ask about the

little copse and the dark rock among the grasses. One person told him that there was no copse but there were grasses, in the park next to the housing development, and there were rocks among the grasses. My father asked how far it was to the park and the man said it was close by—just two hundred yards away—but those two hundred yards were for my father another strenuous journey.

It was dusk by the time he reached the park. The lingering rays of the setting sun illuminated a grassy lawn, and several rocks scattered across the lawn and jutting out of it caught the warm colors of the setting sun. He searched among these rocks for the one he carried in his memory and felt that the dark rock among them looked a lot like the one that I had sat on so many years earlier. He slowly walked over to it and wanted to sit on it, but his body would not obey instructions and kept slipping off, so he could only sit down on the grass and lean his back against the rock. At that moment he realized he lacked the strength to stand up again. His head flopped against the rock and he watched in a powerless daze as a vagrant wearing shabby old clothes rummaged around in a nearby garbage can. The man pulled out a Coke bottle, twisted off the cap, and emptied the remaining drops of soda into his mouth. The vagrant shook the bottle a few more times before tossing it back into the garbage can. Then he turned around and stared at my father like a hawk. My father turned his head away, and when he looked up he found the vagrant was sitting on a bench by the garbage can, his eyes still fixed on him—fixed on his brand-new railway uniform.

"I saw Yang Fei," he told Li Yuezhen, "on that very rock."

He was in his final moments now, and he sank into the darkness as though sinking into a well, with silence all around. The lights in the tall buildings were extinguished and the stars and moon in the sky were extinguished too. Then, all of a sudden, it was as though the scene of my abandonment appeared in a brilliant shaft of light. He saw me, the four-year-old, sitting on the rock in a blue-and-white sailor suit, the one he had bought for me when he decided to give me away. A little sailor boy sat on the dark rock; he was happily waving his legs. "I'm going to get you something to eat," my father said to me sadly. "Dad, be sure to get plenty," I said to him happily.

But this radiant picture vanished in the twinkling of an eye, as a pair of coarse hands forcibly removed his uniform, briefly calling him back from the brink of death. His body was feeling numb, but remaining shreds of consciousness enabled him to realize what the vagrant was doing. The vagrant stripped off the tattered blue clothes he was wearing and put on my father's brand-new uniform.

"Please," my father said weakly. The vagrant bent his head to hear more clearly. "Two hundred yuan," he heard my father murmur. The vagrant groped around in my father's shirt pocket and pulled out two hundred-yuan notes. He transferred them to the breast pocket of the railroad uniform that had been my father's.

"Please," my father said once more. The vagrant stood looking at him for a moment, then squatted down and put the tattered blue jacket on him.

The vagrant heard his last words:

"Thank you."

The darkness was endless. My father sank into a nothingness in which everything was erased, in which he himself was erased. Then it was as though he heard someone calling "Yang Fei!" and his body stood up, and when he stood up he discovered he was walking on an empty and desolate plain, and the person calling "Yang Fei!" was himself. He went on walking and went on calling, "Yang Fei, Yang Fei, Yang Fei, Yang Fei, Yang Fei, Yang Fei, Yang Fei . . ." It was just that the sound of his voice got smaller and smaller. He walked a long way across the plain and didn't know if he had walked for a day or for several days, but his endless calling of my name brought him back to his own city, and his call of "Yang Fei!" seemed to lead him like a road sign to our little shop. He stood on the street outside for a long, long time—two days or two weeks, he could not tell. The doors and windows of the shop remained closed throughout, and I never appeared.

As he stood there, the commonplace sights around him gradually took on an unfamiliar cast, the pedestrians and traffic circulating in the street grew indistinct, and he became aware that the place where he stood was becoming vague and dim. But the shop itself remained clearly recognizable and he continued to stand outside, looking forward to the door opening and me emerging from inside. Finally the door did open, but it was a woman who came out; she turned around and exchanged words with a man inside—a man who was clearly not me. My father bowed his head in disappointment and shuffled off.

"Yang Fei sold the shop and went to look for you," Li Yuezhen told him.

He nodded. "When I saw someone else come out, I knew Yang Fei must have sold the place."

Later, he kept on walking, kept on getting lost, and it was as he puzzled over his location that he heard a nightingale-like song. As he headed toward the source of the music, he saw skeletal people walking this way and that, and as he shuttled among them he entered a wood where the leaves grew bigger and bigger, where swaying babies lay on the broad tree leaves.

The nightingale song was emanating from them. A woman in white approached—he recognized her as Li Yuezhen. She recognized him too, for at this point their looks were unaltered. They stood among the babies that were crooning like nightingales and exchanged accounts of their last moments in that departed world. He asked Li Yuezhen for news of me, and she told him of my visit to his old village—that was all she knew.

Very tired, he lay for several days in the grass beneath the trees, amid the warblings of the twenty-seven babies. Then he stood up, telling Li Yuezhen that he missed me and longed to see my face—even just a glimpse of me in the distance would content him. He resumed his endless journey, continually getting lost on unfamiliar roads, but this time he was unable to return to the city, because he had left that world for too long a time. He could only get as far as the funeral parlor, the interface between the two worlds.

Like me on my first visit there, he entered the waiting room and listened to the crematees as they discussed their burial clothes, cinerary urns, and burial sites, and he watched as one by one they entered the oven room. He stood rather than sat, and soon he came to feel that the waiting room should have a staff member in attendance, for he was someone who loved to work. When a late-arriving crematee entered, he instinctively went to usher him in and get him a number, then led him to a seat. This made him feel a lot like a regular assistant, and he went on walking back and forth in the central aisle. One day he found a pair of old white gloves in the pocket of the tattered blue jacket the vagrant had given him, and after putting them on he felt all the more like a full-time usher. Day after day he showed the utmost courtesy to those awaiting cremation, and day after day he felt an exquisite anticipation, knowing that so long as he kept on doing this, then eventually—in thirty or forty or fifty years—he would be able to see me.

Li Yuezhen paused at this point. I knew now where my father was—he was the man with the blue jacket and the white gloves in the waiting room of the funeral parlor, the man whose face had no flesh but only bone, the man with the weary and grieving voice.

My father had made a point of coming back from the funeral parlor to tell her about his new job, Li Yuezhen added. But he'd left as soon he'd shared this news with her, left in a great hurry, as though he never really should have taken a break.

The sound of Li Yuezhen's voice was like a trickle of water, every word a little water droplet falling to the ground.

THE SIXTH DAY

After many hesitant twists and turns, a young man made his way here, bringing to Mouse Girl news of her boy-friend in that other world.

Looking in dazed confusion at the green grass and the dense trees and the people walking about—many skeletal, some still fleshed—he said to himself, "How did I end up here?"

"It seems like five days now," he went on. "I have been walking around all this time, and I don't know how I ended up here."

A voice piped up. "Some come here just a day after they die, but some take several days."

"I died?" he said perplexedly.

"You didn't go to the funeral parlor?" that same voice asked.

"The funeral parlor?" he asked. "Why would I go there?"

"Everyone has to go to the funeral parlor for cremation after they die."

"You've all been cremated?" He looked at us in wonder. "You don't look like ashes to me."

"We haven't been cremated."

"Did you not go to the funeral parlor, then?"

"No, we've been there."

"If you went, why weren't you cremated?"

"We have no burial grounds."

"I have no burial ground, either," he muttered to himself. "How could I have died?"

"The people who come over after you will tell you," another voice broke in.

He shook his head. "Just now I ran into someone who said he had just got here. He didn't know me and didn't know how I got here, and didn't know how *he* got here, either."

I was about to go over to the cremation waiting room to see my father, but the arrival of this young man made me stop in my tracks. His body looked somehow flattened, with an odd stain on the breast of his jacket. After studying it carefully, I detected the marks left by a car tire.

"Can you remember the final scene?" I asked.

"What final scene?"

"Think about it," I said. "What happened at the end?"

From his expression I could tell he was trying hard to remember. "All I recall was very thick fog as I waited in the street for a bus—I don't remember anything else," he said eventually.

I thought back to that scene in the thick fog when I left my rental room on the first day—how as I passed a bus stop I heard the roar of cars colliding and how one car sped out of the thick fog and then there was a clamor of screams.

"Were you standing next to a bus stop?" I asked.

He thought for a moment. "That's right, I was."

"Did the sign list the 203 bus?"

He nodded. "Yes, it did. The 203 bus was the one I was waiting for."

"It was a car accident that brought you here," I told him. "There's the mark of a car tire on your jacket."

"I died in a car crash?" He lowered his head to look down

at his chest and seemed to understand. "I do seem to remember something knocking me down and running over me."

He looked at me and then at the skeletons close by. "You're different from them," he said.

"I just arrived a few days ago," I said. "They've been here a long time."

"Soon you'll be just like us," one skeleton said.

"Once spring is over—and the summer too," I said. "We'll be just like them."

An uneasy expression appeared on his face. "Does it hurt a lot?" he asked.

"Not at all," the skeleton said. "It's just like tree leaves falling one by one in the autumn wind."

"But a tree will always sprout more leaves," he said.

"We're not going to sprout again," the skeleton said.

He nodded thoughtfully. "I understand."

At this point a woman's voice could be heard. "Xiao Qing!"

"I think someone is calling me," he said.

"Xiao Qing!" the voice called again.

"That's strange. There's someone here who knows me." He looked about in puzzlement.

"Xiao Qing, I'm here."

Mouse Girl was approaching, dressed in a pair of pants so long she was treading on their cuffs. This young man looked at her in astonishment. He had heard her before he saw her.

"Hi, Xiao Qing! I'm Mouse Girl."

"You don't sound like her, but you do look like her."

"I really am Mouse Girl."

"Really?"

"Really."

Mouse Girl came up to us. "How come you're here too?" she asked Xiao Qing.

He pointed at his chest. "Car accident."

Mouse Girl looked at the mark on his jacket. "What's that?"

"A car ran me over," Xiao Qing said.

"Did it hurt a lot?" Mouse Girl asked.

Xiao Qing thought this over. "I don't remember. I may have cried out."

Mouse Girl nodded. "Have you seen Wu Chao?" she asked.

"Yes, I have," he said.

"When was that?"

"The day before I came here."

Mouse Girl turned around and told us that in the world over there Xiao Qing had been another member of the mouse tribe. She and her boyfriend, Wu Chao, had known Xiao Qing for over a year. They were below-ground neighbors.

"Does Wu Chao know what happened to me?"

"Yes, he does," Xiao Qing said. "He bought a burial plot for you."

"He bought a burial plot for me?"

"Yes. He gave me the money and asked me to buy you a burial plot."

"Where did he get the money?"

When Mouse Girl fell to her death, Wu Chao was back home with his father. Later, the old man's condition stabilized, but it was late at night when Wu Chao made it back to the underground rental in the city. He didn't see Mouse Girl and he softly called her name a few times, but there was no answer. Their neighbors were all asleep, so he made his way along the narrow passageway, listening for the sound of human voices, thinking that Mouse Girl perhaps was chatting with someone behind a curtain. He heard nothing but snores and dreamy murmurs and the occasional baby wailing. It occurred to him that Mouse Girl might be in an Internet bar chatting with someone online. As he headed toward the bomb shelter exit he ran into Xiao Qing, just returning from his night shift. Xiao Qing told him of Mouse Girl's death three days earlier.

Wu Chao at first did not seem to react when he heard that Mouse Girl had thrown herself off the Pengfei Tower, but a moment later his whole body started trembling and he kept shaking his head. "That's impossible! Impossible!" he cried, and he dashed toward the exit.

Wu Chao ran into the Internet bar that was closest to the shelter, sat down in front of a computer, and read Mouse Girl's log on QQ space. He also read a news report about her suicide. Now he knew for sure that Mouse Girl had left him forever.

Frozen in shock, he sat in front of the glaring monitor for many minutes, until the screen went black; only then did he get up and leave the Internet bar. When a stranger walked past in the late-night silence, Wu Chao turned to him and said, in a shaky voice, "Mouse Girl is dead."

The stranger gave a start, as though he had run into a lunatic, and quickly crossed to the other side of the street, looking back at him warily.

Wu Chao roamed like a wraith through the night-bound city, in a piercing cold wind. He walked aimlessly, impervious to how far he had gone or where he was, and even when passing the Pengfei Tower he did not raise his head to look. As day broke he still had not emerged from his daze. Among the crowds of jostling people on their way to work, he kept saying over and over again, "Mouse Girl is dead."

His words were greeted with indifference. Only one pedestrian took note of his emotional state and asked him curiously, "Who is Mouse Girl?"

He thought about this blankly for a moment before answering, "Liu Mei." The man shook his head and said he didn't know her, then disappeared around a corner. "She's my girlfriend," Wu Chao muttered.

It was not until the end of the day that Wu Chao returned to his underground home. He lay down distractedly on the bed that he and Mouse Girl used to share. Eventually he fell asleep, but he kept waking up, tears in his eyes.

The next day he neither wept nor sobbed but simply lay in bed, unable to sleep and with no appetite for meals, listening blankly to the sounds of his neighbors stir-frying and chatting and the noise of children running around and shouting. He didn't know what they were doing or what they were saying, and was conscious only of their ebb and flow.

He sank into a deep crevasse of memory, haunted by sudden visions of Mouse Girl, sometimes buoyant, sometimes fretful. Eventually he came to the realization that his most pressing task now was to ensure that she could enjoy proper rest. During her short life she had had many dreams, but practically none of these had he enabled her to fulfill. She had often griped about that, but just as often she had forgotten to gripe, looking forward instead to new prospects. He now felt sure that having a grave of her own must have been her final wish, but this was yet another area in which he seemed likely to fail her.

At this point, amid all the background din, somebody's words carried to him clearly. The man was talking about an acquaintance who had made over thirty thousand yuan from selling a kidney.

Wu Chao sat up in bed, thinking that with that kind of money he could buy a burial plot for Mouse Girl.

He left the bomb shelter and entered the Internet bar. He searched online until he found a phone number. He borrowed a pen and wrote the number on the palm of his hand, then went out to a pay phone and called the number. The person who picked up the phone peppered him with questions until he was sure that Wu Chao was serious, then set up an appointment for them to meet at the Pengfei Tower. Wu Chao couldn't help giving a shiver when he heard the name.

He arrived at the appointed spot to find the street filled with a clamor of cars and people; he and his shadow huddled together at the foot of the Pengfei Tower. One car after another drove into or emerged from the underground parking lot next to him. Several times he looked up at the piercing sunlight reflected from the tower's glass windows, but he had no idea where Mouse Girl had stood that day.

A man in a black down jacket came up to him. "You're Wu Chao?" he muttered.

Wu Chao nodded.

"Follow me," the man said quietly.

They boarded a crowded bus. A few stops later they disembarked, then boarded another bus. After taking six different buses, they seemed to have reached the outskirts of town. Wu Chao accompanied the man to the entrance gate of a housing development. The man told Wu Chao to go on inside, while he stood by the gate and placed a call on his cell phone. As Wu Chao entered this drab development, he noticed a man emerging from a building not far away. The man tossed his cigarette on the ground and stamped it out as Wu Chao approached. "Selling a kidney?" he asked.

Wu Chao nodded. The man beckoned with his hand, indicating he should follow him into the building. They went down a stained concrete staircase to the basement. The man opened a door, and the air was suddenly rank with the odor of stale cigarette smoke. By a dim light Wu Chao could make out seven people inside, sitting on beds, smoking and chatting. Wu Chao headed for the one unoccupied bed.

Wu Chao handed over his ID and signed an agreement to sell a kidney. He was given a medical examination and a blood sample was taken, then he was told to await the result. He began another underground life, sleeping under a greasy quilt, a quilt that looked as though it had never been washed, and that exuded foul smells accumulated from its many previous users. The man who had brought him to the basement visited twice a day, issuing to the men inside packs of cheap cigarettes and two meals—cabbage and potato for lunch, potato and cabbage for dinner. The room had neither tables nor chairs, so they all sat on their beds to eat, apart from two who squatted on their haunches. The fetid odor that wafted through the basement was held in check only when the men were smoking. When they slept, Wu Chao would wake up sometimes, oppressed by such a powerful stench he felt as though his chest were being squeezed.

The other men, all young, chatted idly as they smoked, exchanging notes about conditions at construction sites and factories and moving companies—it seemed they had worked in lots of different places. Making a pot of money quickly was now their goal: even if they were to slave away as coolies for years and years, they said, they would still not be able to make as much money as if they were to sell a kidney. They were looking forward eagerly to life afterward, when they could buy a smart set of clothes, an Apple phone, stay a few nights in a swank hotel, and eat some meals in an upscale restaurant. After indulging in these expectations, they lapsed back into anxiety, for none of the seven had yet received word that he had been successfully matched with an organ recipient, despite waiting here for over a month. One of them had already visited similar outfits in five other cities, and each time had been sent packing within a matter of weeks, on the grounds that nobody wanted his kidney. The kidney vendors would give him only forty-five yuan for traveling expenses, money he would use to buy his way to another kidney-selling operation. He said that he had not a penny to his name, so all he could do was try like a beggar to keep life and limb together, in one kidney-selling den after another.

This man had seen a lot of the world, and when someone complained how tedious the diet was here—just cabbage and potato—he said it couldn't be considered bad, for here you at least got tofu once a week and chicken-bone soup once a week as well. He said he'd stayed in a kidney-selling den where for two months straight he ate disgusting food every day of the week.

Somebody raised a question about the safety of kidney surgery. There was, the kidney-racket veteran announced in a tone of authority, no simple answer to that—it was very much a matter of luck. Kidney vendors, he informed them, were an unscrupulous bunch—people with a conscience wouldn't get involved in this kind of business—and to save money they didn't hire professional surgeons, who would demand a high price for their services; kidney vendors would bring in veterinary surgeons instead.

When they heard it was going to be vets removing their kidneys, the other men were outraged, cursing the damn vendors for jeopardizing their health just so they could maximize profits.

This man took it all in stride, however, saying, "These days there's no shortage of wicked people and outrageous behavior, is there? And besides, a vet still counts as a surgeon, and if he makes a habit of cutting out people's kidneys, he will soon become an old hand and his technique might even be superior to that of a surgeon in a proper hospital."

What outraged *him* was that nobody wanted his kidney. He said he'd had rotten luck the whole time, never once matched with a transplant recipient. Every year, he said, there were a million people suffering from kidney disease who depended on dialysis for survival, but there were only about four thousand legal kidney transplants. How was it possible that nobody wanted his kidney? There should be a million people who need it! The only explanation was that those sons of bitches responsible for matching patient and donor were failing to apply themselves properly to their work, with the result that his perfectly good kidney had gone neglected for almost a year now. If this time, too, he was given his marching orders, he said, he was going first to burn some incense in a temple and beg the bodhisattva to help him sell his kidney in double-quick time, and then get another train ticket and head off to the next kidney-selling den.

Wu Chao said nothing after arriving in the basement, but simply listened indifferently as the men gossiped about this and that, and even when he heard how veterinary surgeons performed the operations, he remained unmoved; it was only when he thought of Mouse Girl that his heart would ache. He prayed that he would be matched successfully as soon as possible, so that he could purchase a burial plot for Mouse Girl with minimum delay. But the seven men in the basement had already been waiting so long, and one had yet to be matched successfully even after almost a year, and this made him deeply anxious. He was stricken with insomnia; on his soiled and smelly bed he tossed and turned, unable to fall asleep.

On Wu Chao's sixth day in the basement, the meal-delivery man appeared at a different time than usual. He opened the door and called, "Wu Chao!"

Before Wu Chao had time to react, the other seven men in the basement looked at each other and realized that none of them had this name—Wu Chao had to be the one who had said not a word since his arrival. "So soon!" they exclaimed.

"Wu Chao, you've got a match," the man at the doorway said.

Wu Chao flung aside the greasy quilt and put on his clothes and shoes under the envious gaze of the other seven. As he walked toward the door, the man who had visited kidney-selling dens in five cities spoke up. "You're a sly one," he said.

Wu Chao followed the meal-delivery man up the stained cement staircase to the fourth floor. The man knocked on a door, and when it was opened, Wu Chao found a middle-aged man sitting on a sofa inside the room. This person greeted Wu Chao warmly and had him sit down next to him, then began to explain that the human body actually requires just one kidney, so the other is redundant—like an appendix, which you can keep or remove as you wish.

Wu Chao was not interested in these issues. "How much will I get for my kidney?" he asked the middle-aged man.

"Thirty-five thousand," the man replied.

Wu Chao thought this sufficient for his purposes, so he nodded.

"We pay top price here," the man said. "Other places pay only thirty."

No need to worry about the surgery, he assured Wu Chao,

for the doctors they used were all from big hospitals and were just taking on these jobs for extra income.

"They say that it's vets who do the operation," Wu Chao responded.

"That's bullshit!" the middle-aged man said, looking displeased. "Our doctors are all fully trained surgeons, and we pay them five thousand for every kidney removal."

Wu Chao moved into a room on the fifth floor. It had four beds, only one of which was occupied. The person there was a man who had already had a kidney removed, and he gave his new roommate a friendly smile, which Wu Chao returned.

This man's operation had been successful, and he was able to prop himself up against the bedstead to talk with Wu Chao. He said he no longer had a fever and would be able to leave in another few days. He asked Wu Chao why he was selling his kidney.

Wu Chao lowered his head in thought. "For my girlfriend," he said.

"Same as me," the other man said.

He had a steady girlfriend back in the countryside, he told Wu Chao. He wanted to marry her, but her parents insisted he needed to have a house first. So he took a job in the city, but the money he made was pitiful—he would need to work nine or ten years before he'd have enough to build a house, and his girlfriend would have married someone else long before that. Selling his kidney was the quickest way to finance the house construction.

"This money comes easy," he said.

He gave a laugh. That's just the way it was back home, he said—if you don't have a house, you can forget about marriage. "Is it the same where you're from?" he asked.

Wu Chao nodded. His eyes suddenly got wet, for he thought of Mouse Girl and how she had stuck with him through thick and thin despite his poverty and failures in life. He bowed his head, not wanting his tears to be seen.

After a moment he raised his head. "Didn't your girlfriend want to leave and get a job in the city as well?"

"She wanted to," the man said, "but her father was bed-ridden and her mother was in poor health too. She's their only daughter—they have no sons—so she can't get away."

Wu Chao thought of Mouse Girl's fate. "Maybe it's better that way."

Life on the fifth floor was a complete contrast to life in the basement. There was no foul air and the quilt was clean. There was natural light. In the morning Wu Chao could eat an egg, a meat bun, and a bowl of congee; at midday and in the evening he ate boxed meals with either meat or fish.

Wu Chao woke up in sunlight and fell asleep by moonlight—sensations long denied him, since for a year or more he had woken and slept in an underground world with neither sun nor moon. Now he appreciated their beauty, and even when he closed his eyes he could feel how they brightened the room. Outside his window was a tree that had turned dry and yellow in the winter cold, but even so, birds would fly over and rest on its limbs, sometimes chirping away, then flapping their wings and soaring over the roof-tops. He thought of Mouse Girl and how she too had never experienced this kind of life during their time together. He couldn't help but feel sad.

Three days later, Wu Chao followed the middle-aged man into a windowless room. A man wearing glasses who looked like he might be a doctor asked him to lie down on a crude operating table. A powerful light shone in his face, and even after he closed his eyes they still felt sore. With the anesthetic, he lost consciousness, and when he came around he found himself lying on his bed on the fifth floor once more. The room was completely silent, for the man who had been there was now gone and Wu Chao was the only occupant. Next to his pillow lay a bag of antibiotics and a bottle of mineral water. At the slightest movement he felt an acute stab of pain in his left side, and he knew he'd lost his left kidney.

The middle-aged man came by twice a day to make sure he took the antibiotics at the proper time. The man told him that he would be able to go back home in a week. Wu Chao lay alone in the room; his only other visitors were the birds. Some would flit past his window, while others would linger briefly on the branches outside, their raucous jabber sounding to his ears like idle chatter.

After a week the middle-aged man gave him thirty-five thousand yuan in cash, summoned a taxi, and sent two of his underlings to see him back to his home in the bomb shelter.

Wu Chao's neighbors, seeing two strangers carry him in and lay him on his bed, knew he must have sold a kidney so that Mouse Girl could get a proper burial.

Wu Chao lay in bed. After a few more days he had finished all the antibiotics, but his high fever had not abated and on several occasions he lapsed into unconsciousness; when he came to, he felt that his body was on the point of leaving him. His underground neighbors came to visit him and bring him snacks, but he was able only to swallow a very little bit of congee or soup. Several neighbors said they should take him to the hospital, but he shook his head emphatically, for he knew that if he was admitted to the hospital he could say goodbye to all the money he made from selling his kidney. He believed he could get through this, but his confidence weakened with every passing day, and as the frequency of his fainting spells increased he knew he wouldn't be fit enough to make the selection of Mouse Girl's burial plot. For this he cried tears of frustration.

Once, Wu Chao woke from unconsciousness and asked in a feeble voice of the neighbors who sat by his side, "Was that a bird?"

"There's no birds," the neighbors said.

"I heard a bird calling," Wu Chao continued weakly.

"I saw a bat on my way here," one of the neighbors said.

"Not a bat," Wu Chao said, "a bird."

Xiao Qing said that the last time he went to see him, Wu Chao found it hard even to open his eyes. It was then that he begged Xiao Qing to help. He told him that there was thirty-five thousand yuan hidden under his pillow and asked him to use thirty-three thousand to buy a burial plot for Mouse Girl, a good-quality tombstone, and an urn for her ashes. The remaining two thousand he said he needed to keep for himself, so that he could come out of this alive and sweep Mouse Girl's grave at the Qingming Festival in future years.

After saying all this, he turned with a moan and had Xiao Qing take the money out from underneath the pillow. The words "The grave of the Mouse Girl I love" were to be carved on the tombstone, he instructed Xiao Qing, with his own name below. Just as Xiao Qing was leaving, money in hand, Wu Chao called him back in a whisper and told him to change "Mouse Girl" to "Liu Mei."

Mouse Girl was weeping. The sound of her sobs spilled over every face and body here, like the patter of rain on plantain leaves. With the twenty-seven babies warbling in the background, her sobs seemed all the more wrenching.

Many of the skeletal people listened raptly and asked each other who was singing, singing so sadly. Others said it wasn't singing but sobbing, it was the pretty girl—the new arrival—who was sobbing, the pretty girl in the man's pants, pants that were long and wide. Every day she'd been walking back and forth and tramping on her pant legs, but now she was sitting on the ground and crying.

Mouse Girl sat amid the riverside greenery, her back against a tree, her legs screened by grass and blossoming wildflowers, the river gurgling close by. As she hummed her song of lamentation, the teardrops on her face looked like morning dew clinging to tree leaves. She was making a dress out of the pair of pants.

Xiao Qing stood close to Mouse Girl. As stationary as a street sign, he watched as skeletal people—and a dozen or more fleshed people—approached from all directions, forming an ever-denser throng. They stood close, listening attentively to Xiao Qing's story. From his expression one could sense that Xiao Qing was on the road to forgetting, for his account was muddled, like an effort to piece together disjointed, incomplete dream sequences.

Everybody came over, excited by the knowledge that Mouse Girl could proceed to her resting place. They talked in hushed voices about how nobody so far had ever left this place and how Mouse Girl was the first, and how, moreover, her body and her beauty were fully intact.

Everyone in this huge crowd was eager to take a closer look at Mouse Girl as she sat sewing her dress among the grasses and beneath the trees, and so they circulated around her, interweaving in an orderly fashion, some pressing forward, others hanging back, like banks of waves forming in the ocean, every one of them blessing with a silent glance this lovely young woman who was about to proceed to her resting place.

An old voice emerged from the crowd that was circling Mouse Girl. "My child, you should bathe," the voice said, as Mouse Girl bowed her head and wept and sewed her dress.

Mouse Girl raised her tear-stained face and looked in astonishment at this skeleton with the old voice.

"Soon you'll be interred," the old voice continued. "So you should bathe now."

"I haven't finished the dress," Mouse Girl said.

"We'll do it for you," many women's voices said.

Dozens of female skeletons came up to Mouse Girl and dozens of pairs of hands reached out to her. Mouse Girl lifted the unfinished dress, unsure into which pair of hands she should place it. "We used to work in a clothing factory," two voices said to her.

Mouse Girl passed them the unfinished dress, then looked up at the old skeleton standing in front of her and asked with some embarrassment, "Can I keep my clothes on?"

The old skeleton shook his head. "You can't bathe if you're dressed."

Mouse Girl lowered her head and in a slow movement let her outer clothes leave her body, then her underwear. When her legs emerged among the grasses and the blossoming wildflowers, she was completely unclothed. Lovely Mouse Girl lay on her back among the grasses and wildflowers, and after putting her legs together she folded her hands across her chest, then closed her eyes, as though entering a dream-like serenity. The grasses and wildflowers growing so profusely around her lowered their heads and bent at the waist as though lost in admiration, their gaze concealing her body from onlookers. Thus she was hidden from view, and we saw only the grasses spreading and the wildflowers blooming.

"People over there make distinctions between family and strangers," the hoary old skeleton continued, "but there are no such demarcations here. With interments over there one needs to be bathed by one's kith and kin, but here we are all her family and we all need to bathe her. People there use bowls of water to bathe a body; here we cup our hands to make a bowl."

Saying this, the old skeleton picked off a tree leaf, cupped it in his hand, and walked over to the stream. The crowd circling Mouse Girl made an orderly line, each one picking a leaf and cupping it in his or her hands, creating a long, long line of cups made of tree leaves, following the old skeleton to the riverside. Like a strand pulled from a ball of thread, they stretched out in a longer and longer arc. The old skeleton was the first to squat down, and after scooping up water in the bowl made by the tree leaf cupped in his hand, he got up and came walking back, and the people who followed him did the same. The old skeleton went up to where Mouse Girl lay, and after opening his hands sprinkled the water from his leaf bowl on top of the grass and wildflowers that covered Mouse Girl's body. The grass and the flowers, sprinkled with the river water, trembled and shook, moistening Mouse Girl.

The old skeleton now began to walk off, holding the wet leaf in his left hand and wiping his eyes with his right, as though wiping away tears when parting from a loved one. Those behind followed suit, walking over to Mouse Girl with their leaf cups and sprinkling her with the cleansing water. They trailed behind the old skeleton, the line of them stretching away into the distance like a serpentine path. Some carried a leaf in their left hand, some in their right, and the leaves dripped their final droplets in the gentle breeze.

The thirty-eight victims of the department store fire had been walking back and forth in a group, but now they separated, each squatting down to scoop up water, then one by one walking over to Mouse Girl and sprinkling the grass and flowers so that her body was washed from head to toe. The little girl began to sob, and so did the little boy, and the other thirty-six gave sympathetic sobs of their own. Although they moved separately, their sobs reminded us that they were a tight-knit group.

Tan Jiaxin and his family were also in this long procession. They too gathered river water in their cupped hands and slowly approached the spot where Mouse Girl lay, and they sprinkled their benediction as Mouse Girl prepared to go to her resting place. As Tan Jiaxin's daughter moved on, she wiped her tears with both hands and her body gave a little tremor; the leaf in her hand drifted to the ground. Where was *her* resting place going to be? she wondered. Tan Jiaxin stretched out an arm and patted her on the shoulder, saying, "So long as everyone is together, one place is as good as another."

Zhang Gang and Li, the two board game enthusiasts and inveterate arguers, also arrived. They piously filled their leaf cups and sprinkled the contents over Mouse Girl's grass-and-flower blanket. Noting a wistful look on Li's face, Zhang Gang patted his skeletal shoulder with his own skeletal hand. "Don't feel you have to wait for me—you can go on ahead, you know," he said.

Li shook his head. "We haven't finished our game."

The crowd of people who had left after bathing Mouse Girl's body now formed several long lines stretching into the distance, while people in other long lines continued to queue up to bathe Mouse Girl—it seemed that this ceremony had a long way to go. Zheng Xiaomin's parents also arrived, her mother still ill at ease, huddling herself up, her hands on her thighs, her father sticking close to his wife, hugging her as though eager to cover her. They separated, however, to pick leaves and scoop up water, and then the man, closely followed by his wife, led the way, as they moved along in the queue.

Again the nightingale song burst forth, but only in brief snatches. Li Yuezhen walked over slowly in her white clothes, with the twenty-seven babies forming a line and singing as they followed behind her. Perhaps the grass was tickling the babies' necks, for giggles often interrupted their beautiful song. Li Yuezhen carried the babies one by one to the broad tree leaves beside the river. As the babies lay on the leaves that swayed in the breeze, their song was no longer intermittent, but flowed freely like the river water itself.

Mouse Girl, surrounded by grass and flowers, heard the nightingale chorus rising and falling on all sides, and without conscious effort she began to sing the babies' song. Mouse Girl became the lead member of the choir. She would sing a line and the babies would follow; she would sing another line and they would follow that; and the lead and the chorus would repeat themselves over and over, as though they had rehearsed this in advance, and Mouse Girl's and the babies' songs rose and fell, rose and fell.

My footsteps, originally heading on a path toward the funeral parlor, toward my father, still lingered here.

THE SEVENTH DAY

I have never been so clean as I am now," Mouse Girl said. "I feel almost transparent."

"We have bathed you."

"I know, many of you have done that."

"Not many of us—all of us."

"It felt as though all the water in the river was washing me clean."

"Everyone lined up to bathe you."

"You're so good to me."

"Here we're good to everyone."

"And you're seeing me off as well."

"You're the first to leave here to rest."

We walked along the road, thronging around Mouse Girl as she proceeded to the funeral parlor. The road was a broad wilderness, so long and wide you could not see its end, as vast as the sky above our heads.

"When I was over there," said Mouse Girl, "I liked spring best, and hated winter. Winter was too cold, so cold it made my body shrink, whereas in spring the flowers blossomed— and my body bloomed as well. But here I like the winter and was dreading the spring, thinking my body would rot when spring arrived. But now everything's fine—I don't need to worry about the spring."

"Even if spring were to move as fast as an Olympic sprint champion can run in the world over there, it wouldn't be able to catch up with you," one of us said.

Mouse Girl chuckled.

"You're so pretty," another said.

"You're saying that to please me, aren't you?" Mouse Girl responded.

"You really are pretty," we assured her.

"When I walked down the street over there, they would turn their heads to look at me. Now, over here, you turn around to look at me too."

"It's called a high head-turn rate."

"You're right—that's what they call it over there."

"That's what we call it over here too."

Mouse Girl chuckled once more. "There and here, everyone calls it a high head-turn rate."

"The head-turn rate goes wherever you do," we said.

"You're sweet-talking me!"

Mouse Girl was wearing the dress she had made out of the pair of pants. The dress was so long that we couldn't see her feet—all we could see was her dress trailing along the ground.

"The way your dress trails along the ground," someone said, "it looks like a wedding dress."

"Really?" she asked.

"Really," we answered.

"You're just saying that to humor me, aren't you?"

"Not at all, it really looks like a wedding dress."

"But I'm not going off to get married."

"It looks like that, though."

"I'm not wearing makeup, and brides always doll themselves up."

"You may not be wearing makeup, but you're more dazzling than any woman in makeup over there."

"I'm not going off to marry Wu Chao." A melancholy note crept into Mouse Girl's voice. "I'm going to my burial place to rest."

Mouse Girl's tears began to flow, and we fell silent.

"I was too impulsive," she said. "I shouldn't have left him."

She walked on with a heavy heart, saying dejectedly, "How will he manage by himself? It was I who got him into this."

Mouse Girl wept as she made the long trek across the open country.

"I often got him into trouble," she said. "When we were hairwashers in the salon, he had his sights set on something better, so he sought advice from the stylist on how to cut hair. He learned so quickly that the manager praised him and said he planned to have him be a hairdresser. Privately Wu Chao told me that once he officially became a hairdresser he'd make a better income, and once he was really proficient he would quit the job and the two of us would rent a space and open up a little salon of our own. There was a girl in the salon who liked him and was always sidling up to him and coming on strong. This got me mad, and I'd give her a hard time every chance I got. Once, we actually started to fight. She grabbed my hair and I grabbed hers, and Wu Chao came over to pull us apart. I shouted at him and asked him if he wanted her or wanted me and got him very embarrassed. I yelled at him so loud that all the clients in the salon turned around to look at me. The manager was furious and told me to clear the hell out. While the manager was still cursing me, Wu Chao went up to him and announced that we were both handing in our notice and told the guy he was an asshole, then came back and put his arm around me and led me out of the salon. I said we still had two weeks' wages due, and he said the hell with that, I don't give a shit. That drove me to tears. We walked down the street for a long time, him with his arm around me, and all along I was crying and saying I'd let him down and made him lose face and wrecked his future, because he was just about to become a hairdresser. He had one hand around me and kept wiping away my tears with the other, saying, 'The hell with being a hairdresser, the hell with losing face, I couldn't care less about any of that!'

"Later I suggested we look for work at another salon, given that he already had mastered the skills of a hairdresser, but he refused. I promised not to get jealous again and told him if another girl took a fancy to him I'd just ignore it, but he insisted there was no way he would work in a salon. So the only option was to work in a restaurant. The manager said since I was good-looking he'd have me serve in an upstairs private room, while Wu Chao could service the large dining room downstairs. The manager liked how dedicated and nimble he was, and it wasn't long before Wu Chao was promoted to captain. In free moments he would go chat with the chef and pick up some cooking tips. Once he'd really learned the ropes, he told me, we'd quit and set up our own little restaurant.

"It was often businessmen and officials who booked the private room. There was one time when a whole bunch of them had a bit too much to drink, and one put his arms around me and started squeezing my boobs. I shouldn't have made an issue of it, I should just have found an excuse to leave the room, but I ran downstairs sobbing to complain to Wu Chao. He could never tolerate anyone taking advantage of me, so he barged into the private room and started a fight. He was way outnumbered, and they got him down on the ground and started kicking him, kicking him in the head. It was only when I threw myself on top of him and begged them to stop that they finally left him alone. The restaurant manager came up and bowed and scraped and apologized to them. They had been the ones doling out abuse, but the manager didn't stand up for us at all and cursed us out instead. Wu Chao's face was covered in blood. I put my arms around him and helped him out of the private room, but once we got downstairs he pushed me aside, wanting to go back upstairs and fight another round. He only made it up a few steps before I dashed over and clung to one of his legs for dear life, crying and begging him not to. He came back down and helped me to my feet, and we left the restaurant clinging to each other. His nose was bleeding the whole time, and it was raining outside, and when we got to the other side of the road he didn't want to go any farther, so he sat down on the sidewalk and I sat next to him. The rain poured down, drenching our clothes, and cars kept driving past and splashing us with the water from the puddles. 'I want to kill someone!' he said again and again, and I just couldn't stop crying, begging him to calm down.

"Once more I'd ruined things for him—he never got to be a chef, and now we were never going to be able to open a restaurant. For two months we didn't go to work. We never had much money in the first place, and now we could just eat one meal a day, and after two months of that our money was almost gone. We needed to find jobs, I said, but he refused—he said he wasn't going to take any more abuse. I said that if we don't have jobs we don't have money, and without money all we can do is to wait around until we die of hunger. Even if it means we die of hunger, he said, I refuse to be pushed around. I wept, wept with heartbreak, not because I was angry with him but because the world is so unjust. Seeing me weep, he went out, and it was very late that night when he got back, bringing me two big, steaming-hot stuffed buns. Where did he get the money to buy these buns? I asked. He had spent the day collecting discarded cans and plastic bottles and selling them to a recycler, he said. When he left the room the next day, I went out with him. Why are you coming with me? he asked. To pick up bottles and cans with you, I said."

"It looks like we're there."

We had all walked a long road and now we had arrived at the funeral parlor. As we swarmed inside, a hum of amazement arose in the waiting room. Seeing so many skeletons crowding in, the crematees turned to one another in confusion. "What are these things, and why have they come here?"

"I guess they just got here late," one among the plastic chairs said.

"They got here way too late," someone else said.

"They're fucking old, these ones!" someone in one of the armchairs exclaimed.

"We're vintage spirits," one of us muttered, "and they're draft beer." A wave of titters rose from the line of skeletons.

There were a dozen or so crematees seated in the ordinary section of plastic chairs, and only three in the elite armchair zone. Several skeletons walked over to the armchairs, struck by how spacious and comfortable it seemed there. The man in the faded blue jacket and the grubby old white gloves approached and said wearily, "That's the VIP zone. Please sit over here."

His empty eyes suddenly saw me, and both delight and consternation rose and fell in his glance. This time he recognized me, because Li Qing's hand had restored my face to its original shape.

I wanted to greet him with a gentle "Dad," and my mouth opened, but no sound came out. I felt that he too wanted to greet me, but he made no sound either.

Then I felt the sad expression in his eyes as he asked with a trembling voice, "Is it you?"

I shook my head and pointed at Mouse Girl. "No. Her."

He seemed to give a long sigh of relief, as though temporarily released from sorrow. He nodded, went and collected a slip of paper from the number dispenser by the entrance, then walked back and handed it to Mouse Girl. I saw that the number A53 was printed on it. He studied me carefully, and I heard a deep sigh as he walked away.

We sat down on the plastic chairs.

Mouse Girl gripped her ticket earnestly, for it was her passport to the place of rest. "Finally I'm going there."

We felt that the whole waiting room was enveloped in a certain emotion, an emotion that Mouse Girl then expressed. "How is it I'm so reluctant to leave?"

We felt another emotion form, and this one too Mouse Girl expressed. "Why do I feel so upset?"

We felt there was one other emotion, and this too Mouse Girl put into words. "I should be happy."

"That's right," we said. "You should be happy."

No smile appeared on Mouse Girl's face, for a matter of concern now occupied her mind. "When I leave," she instructed, "please don't any of you look at me, and when you leave here, please don't look back. That way I can forget you and find true rest."

We nodded in unison, the way leaves rustle in the wind.

Number A43 was called, and from one of the plastic chairs

in front of us a man in a cotton Mao-jacket burial suit rose to his feet and shuffled off. We sat quietly, and as late-arriving cremates continued to enter, the usher in the faded blue jacket and worn white gloves greeted them and picked up numbers, then conducted them to the plastic seating.

All was quiet among the plastic chairs, but a hum of conversation could be heard coming from the armchairs. Three VIPs were discussing their expensive burial outfits and luxurious burial sites. One of them was wearing a fur burial robe, and the other two were quizzing him about the need for it.

"I can't stand cold," he explained.

"It's not actually cold there," one of the others observed.

"That's true," the third chipped in. "The winters are mild and the summers cool."

"Who says it's not cold?"

"That's what the feng shui masters say."

"No feng shui master has ever been there, so how would they know?"

"It doesn't necessarily follow. You may not have eaten pork, but you've probably seen a pig run around."

"Eating pork and seeing a pig are completely different things. I've never set any store by that feng shui business."

The other two fell silent. "Nobody who's gone there has ever come back," the man in the fur robe said, "so nobody knows whether it's hot or cold. If by any chance the conditions are harsh, I'm all prepared."

"He doesn't understand," a skeleton near me muttered. "Fur comes from animals. He's going to be reborn an animal."

The other two VIPs asked the man in the fur robe where his burial site was. On a tall mountain peak, they were told, and one where the mountain falls away on all sides, so that he could enjoy a 360-degree view.

The other two VIPs nodded. "Excellent choice."

"They don't have a clue," the same skeleton muttered. "A mountain should have high spurs on both sides rather than fall away sheer. If it has high spurs, one's children will prosper, but if it falls away on both sides, one's children will end up beggars."

The number V12 was now called. The VIP in the fur robe rose with a slight stoop, as though from extensive experience of emerging from sedan cars. He nodded to his two peers, then walked smugly toward the oven room.

It was now the turn of A44. The number was slowly called three times, and then it was on to A45. This number too was called slowly three times, and then it was on to A46. When the numbers were called, it was like the sound of soughing wind on a dark night—drawn out and lonely. This lonesome sound made the waiting room seem empty and unreal. After three unanswered summonses, A47 stood up—a female figure who came forward hesitantly.

We sat quietly around Mouse Girl, conscious that the hour of her leaving was growing closer. After the VIPs V13 and V14 left, the call went out for A52 and our eyes could not help but turn toward Mouse Girl. She sat lost in thought with her hands clasped in front of her chest, her head bowed.

After A52 was called three times, we heard Mouse Girl's A53 called and we bowed our heads in unison, conscious that Mouse Girl was walking away from the plastic chairs.

Although I had averted my gaze, I could still in my imagination see Mouse Girl, trailing a wedding-gown-like dress behind her, walking off to her resting place. I could see her walk off but did not see the oven room and did not see the burial ground. What I saw was her walking toward a place where ten thousand flowers bloom.

Then I heard the plastic seats give a slight creak and I knew the skeletons were rising from their places and leaving, withdrawing gently, the way a tide goes out.

I stayed put. In the row in front of me, five remaining cremates were seated, and my father in his faded blue jacket and worn white gloves stood in the passageway to their left, looking ready to respond to any need they might have. I felt as though my father's erect figure was like that of a silent mourner. When a crematee turned his head and said something, my father stepped forward promptly and responded quietly to the person's question, then withdrew to his post in the passageway. My father was always sedulous in performing his duties, no matter whether in that departed world or in this one.

After the remaining five crematees entered the oven room in turn, the waiting room seemed so empty it was almost as though it had run out of air, with only a dim light emanating from the widely separated candle-shaped sconces. My father came over with heavy steps and I rose to meet him. I clutched his empty sleeves—the bones inside seemed as slender as a cord. Supporting his weight, I was planning to head toward the VIP zone, where comfortable chairs awaited. But my father stopped me, saying, "That's not the place for us."

We sat down on the plastic chairs and I clasped my father's gloved hand. Through a hole in the glove I could feel the bones of his fingers, and they seemed so brittle that they would break at the slightest impact. My father's dim eyes peered at me as though determined to confirm my identity. "You're here so soon," he said mournfully.

"Dad," I said, "were you afraid of being a burden, and that's why you left?"

He shook his head. "I just wanted to go back there and have a look," he said.

"Why?"

"I was upset. The thought of having abandoned you upset me."

"Dad," I said, "you didn't abandon me."

"I just thought of that rock, and wanted to sit there for a bit. I'd always wanted to go there. When it got dark, I would want to go there, but in the morning I would see you and change my mind, because I couldn't bear to leave you."

"Dad, why didn't you tell me? I would have gone with you."

"I thought of telling you—I thought of that many times."

"So why didn't you?"

"I don't know."

"Were you worried I'd be upset?"

"No, that wasn't it," he said. "I preferred to go there myself."

"So you left without saying goodbye."

"No," he said, "I meant to come back on the evening train."

"But you didn't."

"I did." After he died, he meant. "I stood a long time opposite the shop and saw it was someone else who came out from inside."

"I went to look for you."

"When I saw that someone else had taken over the shop, I knew you had gone to look for me."

"I kept looking and looking," I said. "I went to the department store, because there had been a fire there the day you left and I worried you might have been trapped."

"What department store?"

"The big silver one not far from the shop."

"I don't remember that."

I realized that when the department store opened he was already struck down by illness and pain. "You never went there," I said.

"You're here so soon," he repeated.

"I looked all over the city, and I went to the countryside to look for you too," I said.

"Did you see your uncles and aunts?" he asked.

"I saw them, yes. There's a lot of change there too." I didn't tell him how desolate things looked.

"Do they still bear a grudge?" he asked.

"No, they were very upset by the news."

"I should have gone to see them long ago," he said.

"I looked for you everywhere," I said. "It just never occurred to me that you had taken the train there."

"I boarded the train—" he muttered.

I smiled, thinking how we had been looking for each other in two separate worlds.

Once more he picked up his mournful refrain: "You're here so soon."

"Dad, I never thought I would find you here."

"Every day here I was hoping to see you, but I didn't want you to come so soon."

"Dad, we're together now."

After a long parting, my father and I had run into each other again. Although we now had no body warmth and no breath, we were together once more. I removed my hand from the slender, bony fingers inside his old glove and carefully placed it on his bony shoulder. I very much wanted to say "Dad, come with me." But I knew he loved to work, loved this waiting-room usher's work, so I simply said, "Dad, I'll often come visit you."

I felt a smile appear on his skeletal face.

"Does your birth mother know?"

"Not yet, I don't think."

He gave a sigh. "They'll find out before long."

I said nothing more, and he said nothing either. The waiting room fell back into the quiet of remembrance. We treasured this moment of togetherness and in silence felt each other's presence. I was conscious that he was gazing intently at the scars on my face. Li Qing had only restored my left eye, nose, and chin, without erasing the scars left there.

His hands, encased in those old white gloves, began to rub my shoulders. His skeletal fingers were trembling, and I felt his caress was designed to signal a reunion just as much as a final parting.

His fingers froze when they reached my black armband. He hung his head, sinking into a distant grief. He knew that after he left I had become a lonely orphan in that other world. He did not inquire what events had led to my arrival here, perhaps because he didn't want to upset me, or perhaps because he didn't want to upset himself. After a little while he told me softly that he wanted to wear the armband. This was genuinely his wish, I could tell, so I nodded and took it off and passed it to him. He removed his gloves, and ten trembling skeletal fingers received the armband. He placed it on his empty sleeve.

After he put the worn white gloves back on his skeletal hands, he raised his head to look at me, and I saw two tears fall from his empty eyes. Although he had arrived here before me, he still shed the tears that white-haired people shed for dark-haired ones.

On my way back, a young man hailed me. His left hand clutching his midriff, he was walking in haste but with a slight stoop, as though still recovering from a major illness. "Somebody told me that if I keep going in this direction I can see my girlfriend," he said to me.

"Who's your girlfriend?" I asked.

"The prettiest girl around."

"What's her name?"

"Her name's Liu Mei. She's also called Mouse Girl."

"You must be Wu Chao," I said. A fur hat now covered his unruly hair. It must have been a long time since he had dyed his hair, or cut it.

"How do you know that?"

"I recognize you."

"Where have we met?"

"In the shelter."

My reminder gradually cleared away the confusion on his face. "I do feel I've seen you somewhere."

"Yes, in the shelter."

Now he remembered, and the wisp of a smile appeared on his face. "That's right, that's where I saw you."

I looked at the area on his waist that his left hand was clutching. "Is it still sore there?"

"Not anymore," he said.

His hand left the spot, only to return to the same place out of habit soon after.

"We know you sold a kidney to buy a burial plot for Mouse Girl," I said.

"We?" he looked at me in confusion.

"Me and the others over there." I pointed up ahead.

"The others over there?"

"Those of us without graves."

He nodded, seeming to have understood. "How do you know about me?" he asked.

"Xiao Qing came over, and he told us."

"Xiao Qing's here too?" he said. "When did he come?"

"It must be six days ago now," I said. "He kept getting lost and didn't get here until yesterday."

"How did he come over?"

"A traffic accident—it happened in the thick fog."

"I don't know anything about fog," he said, perplexed.

He couldn't have known, I realized, recalling that Xiao Qing had said Wu Chao was lying in the underground bomb shelter the whole time.

"You were in the bomb shelter then," I said.

He nodded, then asked, "How long have you been here?"

"This is my seventh day," I said. "How about you?"

"It seems to me I just came over," he replied.

"Today, in other words." I realized that he and Mouse Girl had just missed each other.

"You must have seen Mouse Girl." An expectant look appeared on his face.

"I did." I nodded.

"Was she happy?"

"She was," I said. "But when she realized you had sold a kidney to buy her a burial plot, she wept. She wept her heart out."

"Is she still crying now?"

"Not anymore."

"I'll be able to see her very soon."

Joy appeared on his face like the shadow of a tree leaf.

"You won't be able to see her," I said after a moment of hesitation. "She has gone to rest."

"She's left for there already?"

The joyful shadow left his face, to be replaced by a shadow of grief.

"When did she leave?" he asked.

"Today," I said. "Just as you were coming over, she left. You missed each other."

He lowered his head and walked on, weeping silently. After walking some distance, he stopped weeping. "If I'd just come a day earlier," he said sorrowfully, "that would have been perfect—I could have seen her then."

"If you'd come a day earlier," I said, "you would have seen a dazzling Mouse Girl."

"She was always dazzling," he said.

"She was all the more dazzling on the way to the place of rest," I said. "She wore a long dress like a wedding dress, which trailed along the ground—"

"She doesn't have such a long dress. I've never seen her in such a dress," he said.

"It was a dress made from a pair of man's pants," I explained.

"I see. I heard that her jeans split—I read about it on the Internet," he said mournfully. "She must have worn some-one else's pants."

"Some kind person dressed her in them."

We walked on in silence. The empty plain was absolutely still, making us feel that our walking was simply walking in place.

"Was she happy?" he asked me. "Was she happy as she went off in her long dress?"

"She was happy," I said. "She was happy that you had bought her a burial plot and that before the winter was out she could go to rest, taking her beauty with her. We told her she looked like a bride going off to her wedding. When she heard this she cried."

"Why did she cry?" he asked.

"She thought of how she wasn't going off to marry you, but going to rest at her burial spot. That's what made her cry."

Wu Chao was distressed. As he walked on, he rubbed his eyes with both hands.

"I shouldn't have deceived her," he said. "I shouldn't have tried to fob off a fake iPhone on her. She was so keen to have an iPhone and would talk about this every day. She knew I was broke and couldn't afford a real iPhone—it was all just fantasy talk. I shouldn't have tried to fool her with a fake. I understand why she wanted to take her own life—it wasn't that I'd bought her a knockoff, but that I hadn't come clean with her."

He lowered his hands. "If I'd said to her that this is a knockoff, because it's all I can afford, she would have been pleased, she would have thrown herself into my arms and hugged me, knowing I'd done everything I could.

"She was so good to me, staying with me for three years, three years of hardship. Being poor made us quarrel. Often I lost my temper, cursing her or beating her. I feel terrible when I think about it, for I should never have lost control like that. No matter how poor or hard our life was, she never once mentioned leaving me—it was only when I was mean to her that she wept and threatened to leave me, but after crying she still stayed on.

"She had a girlfriend who was an escort at a nightclub, turning tricks every night, and the girlfriend could make tens of thousands a month, so Mouse Girl wanted to work at the nightclub too, because if she just did that for a few years she'd make enough money to go back home with me and build a house and get married—marrying me was her greatest wish, she said. I said no, I wouldn't tolerate other men touching her, and I beat her, beat her that time till her face swelled up and she wept and screamed that she was going to leave me. But she woke up the next morning and hugged me and said sorry to me over and over again, saying she would never let another man put his hand on her, even if I died she wouldn't let another man touch her, she would live as a widow. We're not married yet, I said, and if I die you don't count as a widow. She said that's crap, if you die I'm your widow.

"Last winter was even colder than this one, and after we moved into the bomb shelter we'd spent all the money we had and had yet to find new work, so we lay for a day in bed and just drank some hot water, hot water she'd got from a neighbor. In the evening we were so hungry it was driving us mad, and she got out of bed and got dressed and said she was going out to beg for some food. How are you going to do that? I asked. Stand in the street and beg, she said. I said no, that's begging. She said if you don't want to, then just stay in bed, I'll go and get something for you to eat. I wouldn't let her leave. I'm not going to be a beggar, I said, and I'm not going to let you be one, either. We're starving, she said, who gives a shit about being a beggar or not? She insisted, so I had no choice but to put on a jacket and follow her out of the bomb shelter.

"It was freezing that night and the wind was strong, gusting down our necks and chilling us to the bone. The two of us stood in the street and she would say to people as they came up, we haven't eaten all day, can you give us a little money? Nobody paid us the slightest attention. We stood in the icy wind for over an hour, and she said, this is no way to beg, we need to wait outside the door of a restaurant. She took my hand and we walked past a brightly lit bakery, and she turned around and walked me back and told me to stand outside the door while she went in. Through the window I saw her say something to the girl behind the counter and the girl shook her head; then she went over to people sitting there eating baked goods and drinking hot drinks and said something to them, and they too shook their heads. I knew that they were refusing to give her bread. She came out of the shop as though nothing had happened, then took my hand and led me to the entrance of what looked like a very posh restaurant, and she said, let's wait here: when the people inside have finished eating and come out with boxed leftovers, we can ask them to give us stuff. By this time I was both cold and hungry and could hardly stand up straight in the bitter wind, but she seemed to be neither cold nor hungry, standing there watching one group of diners after another as they emerged from the restaurant. None of them seemed to be carrying leftovers, and one car after another pulled over and took them away. The place was just too ritzy, and everyone who ate there had lots of money and none of them would have dreamt of taking their leftovers home.

"Later a guy who looked like a businessman was saying goodbye to some people who looked like officials, and then he stood at the door of the restaurant talking on the phone to his driver, so she went up to him and said, We haven't eaten all day, but we're not begging, we're not asking for money, we're just asking that you do us the kindness of going to the bakery next door and buying us a couple of loaves of bread. The man put away his phone and looked at her, saying, A girl as pretty as you can't rustle up a couple of loaves of bread? You can't eat your looks, she said. The guy laughed and said, It's true you can't eat your looks, but they're intangible assets, at least. Intangible assets are empty, she said, but bread is real. Hey, the guy went, you're smart as well as pretty, why don't you come with me, I'll feed you anything you like. She turned around and pointed at me, saying, I'm spoken for. The guy looked at me as if to say, that little down-and-out!

"The guy's Mercedes came over and he opened the door and said to the driver, go over to the bakery and get four loaves of bread. The driver got out and trotted over to the bakery. The guy's phone rang and he picked it up. His driver ran back with the bread, and as he talked on the phone the man said to the driver, Give it to them. The driver gave her the bag of bread, and she said, Thanks. The guy got into his Mercedes and the car drove off. Her hand reached into the bag and broke off a piece of freshly baked bread and popped it into my mouth, then she put the bag inside her jacket. Her ice-cold hand took my ice-cold hand and she said to me, 'Let's go back home to eat.'

"We returned to our underground home and she went over to a neighbor's to ask for a cup of hot water. We sat on the bed and she had me first drink some hot water, before eating the bread—she was afraid I might choke. She was beaming with pleasure as though we had nothing more to worry about. As I was eating, I suddenly burst into tears, but I swallowed my tears as I swallowed the bread, saying to her, we'd still better separate, best not to keep suffering with me. She put down the loaf she was eating and tears spilled from her eyes. Don't even dream of dumping me, she said, I plan to stick with you all my life—even if I die and become a ghost I will still stick with you.

"She was so pretty and was pursued by so many men, all of whom made better money than me, but she steeled herself to live in poverty with me. Sometimes she would complain, complain that she'd chosen the wrong guy, but that was just talk, and after she said it she would forget she was with the wrong guy."

A smile appeared on Wu Chao's face. We had already walked a long way and on all sides was still an empty plain; we were walking on in isolation. A sweet smile now appeared on Wu Chao's face—he was talking about the scene when he first met Mouse Girl.

"When I saw Mouse Girl for the first time three years ago, she was washing hair in a salon. I just happened to pass by and casually glance into the salon, and I saw Mouse Girl standing by the door and greeting clients. She looked at me too, and my heart started pounding right there and then, for I'd never seen such a pretty girl before—when her eyes rested on me it was as though she was stealing my soul. I walked ahead some twenty yards but couldn't go any farther. I hesitated for a long time, then walked back, to find her still standing at the door. When I gazed at her, she gave me another look, and that look was enough to make my heart jump. After passing, I hesitated once more, and when I walked back again, the girl at the door to welcome clients was not Mouse Girl anymore. Mouse Girl was inside washing someone's hair. Through the window I saw her face in a mirror, and she saw me in the mirror and gave me the once-over.

"After four times back and forth in front of the salon, I summoned up the courage to go inside. The girl by the door thought I had come to get my hair cut and said, Welcome. I stammered out a question, Is the manager in? A man standing by the cash register said, I'm the manager. Do you need a hairwasher? I asked. Not just now, he said. But the salon opposite is looking for someone, you could try there.

"I walked out of the salon rather forlornly, not daring to look Mouse Girl in the eyes. I walked for ages but simply couldn't get her out of my mind. A couple of days later, I summoned up the courage to go in again and ask the manager if he needed a hairwasher. Again the manager suggested I try the salon opposite. In the month that followed I went back every week, and each time I felt that Mouse Girl was looking at me. The fourth time, as luck would have it, a male hairwasher had quit and I was able to fill his position. His work number had been 7, so now I was Number 7. Mouse Girl threw me a glance and her face twisted into a grin.

"On my first evening at the salon there weren't many customers getting their hair done, so Mouse Girl sat in a chair flipping through a hairdressing magazine, occasionally raising her head and fluffing her hair in the mirror, as though contemplating different options. I sat down in the chair next to hers, and because I was nervous I was wheezing for breath, so Mouse Girl turned to me and said, 'You got asthma?' I hastily shook my head, and said no, I didn't have asthma. 'Your wheezing is scary,' she said.

"I got more and more tense the longer I sat next to her, worried that my wheezing sounded like asthma, and I breathed carefully, as though holding my breath underwater. She kept flipping through the hairdressing magazine and experimenting with different hairstyles. Finally I summoned up the courage to ask, 'What's your name?'

" 'Number 3,' she said, not even raising her head.

"Her tone was frosty, and I felt deflated. But a moment later she raised her head and looked at me with a smile. 'What's *your* name?' she asked.

" 'Number 7,' I said in a fluster.

"She chuckled. 'What's Number 7's name?' she asked.

"Only then did I remember my name. 'Number 7 is called Wu Chao.'

"She closed her magazine. 'Number 3 is called Liu Mei,' she said."

Wu Chao broke off his account and came to an abrupt halt as he gazed at the view before him. A look of awe appeared on his face, for now he saw for the first time the scene that had made such an impression on me—streams flowing, grass covering the ground, trees in luxuriant growth, with fruit hanging from their branches and heart-shaped leaves that fluttered to a heartbeat rhythm. And people—some fully fleshed, many just bones—were strolling at leisure, back and forth.

He turned to me in astonishment, and his perplexed expression seemed to be posing an inquiry.

"Go on over," I said to him. "The tree leaves there will beckon you, the rocks will smile to you, the river will greet you. There's no poverty here and no riches; there's no sorrow and no pain; no grievances and no hate. . . . Here everyone finds equality in death."

"What's the name of this place?" he asked.

"The land of the unburied."

CHRONICLE OF A BLOOD MERCHANT

One of the last decade's ten most influential books in China, this internationally acclaimed novel by one of the mainland's most important contemporary writers provides an unflinching portrait of life under Chairman Mao. A cart-pusher in a silk mill, Xu Sanguan augments his meager salary with regular visits to the local blood chief. His visits become lethally frequent as he struggles to provide for his wife and three sons at the height of the Cultural Revolution. Shattered to discover that his favorite son was actually born of a liaison between his wife and a neighbor, he suffers his greatest indignity, while his wife is publicly scorned as a prostitute. Although the poverty and betrayals of Mao's regime have drained him, Xu Sanguan ultimately finds strength in the blood ties of his family. With rare emotional intensity, grippingly raw descriptions of place and time, and clear-eyed compassion, Yu Hua gives us a stunning tapestry of human life in the grave particulars of one man's days.

Fiction

ANCHOR BOOKS
Available wherever books are sold.
www.anchorbooks.com